TRAIL OF HOPE

BOOK ONE

HEIDI VANLANDINGHAM

SHADOWHEART PRESS

Trail of Hope is a work of fiction. Names, characters, places, and incidents are the product of the author's imagination or are used fictitiously. Any resemblance to actual events, locales, or persons, living or dead, is purely coincidental.

Trail of Hope: © 2017 by Heidi Vanlandingham

Previously published by The Wild Rose Press ©2013

Contact: Heidi@heidivanlandingham.com

Cover design © EDHGraphics

ISBN: 978-1977984159

All rights reserved. No part of this book may be reproduced in any form or by any electronic or mechanical means, including information storage and retrieval systems, without written permission from the author, except for the use of brief quotations in a book review.

ALSO BY HEIDI VANLANDINGHAM

IN READING ORDER

For all Buy Links: www.heidivanlandingham.com

Western Trails

Trail of Hope

Trail of Courage

Trail of Secrets

Mia's Misfits

Mia's Misfits is also in ABC Mail-Order Bride series

Trail of Redemption

American Mail-Order Bride series &
Prequel to Mail-Order Brides of the Southwest

Lucie: Bride of Tennessee

Mail-Order Brides of the Southwest

The Gambler's Mail-Order Bride

The Bookseller's Mail-Order Bride

The Marshal's Mail-Order Bride

The Woodworker's Mail-Order Bride

The Gunslinger's Mail-Order Bride

The Agent's Mail-Order Bride

WWII

Heart of the Soldier

Flight of the Night Witches

Night Witch Reborn: Natalya

The Peacemaker: Aleksandra

The Warrior Queen: Raisa

The Last Night Witch: Lilyann

Kingdom of the Elf Lords

Return of the Elf Lord

Coming 2022

The Elf Lord's Curse

Of Mystics and Mayhem

In Mage We Trust

Saved By the Spell

The Curse That Binds

Mistletoe Kisses

Music and Moonlight

Sleighbells and Snowflakes

Angels and Ivy

Nutcrackers and Sugarplums

Box Sets Available

Mail-Order Brides of the Southwest: 3-Book collection

Mistletoe Kisses: 4-book collection

Western Trails: 2-book collection

If you love historical romances, sign up for my reader list, and as a thank you, I'll send you the prequel book, a novella, in my Western Trails series.

To download, go to http://tiny.cc/nl-histwest

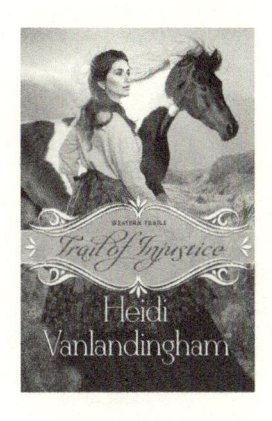

PRAISE FOR TRAIL OF HOPE

"*TRAIL OF HOPE*" is about good vs. evil and characters with the strength and resilience to overcome adversity in a hopeless world. Heidi Vanlandingham weaves these elements together in a vivid, beautifully written love story you won't want to miss."
~*Alicia Dean, author of* **The Isle of Fangs series**

"Debut author Heidi Vanlandingham richly captures historic details in this exciting romance about a woman who only wants a family and a man sworn to vengeance. As they struggle to survive the Trail of Tears, their journey becomes a trail of hope. Vanlandingham is a terrific new voice."
~*Silver James, author of* **Red Dirt Royalty** *by Harlequin*

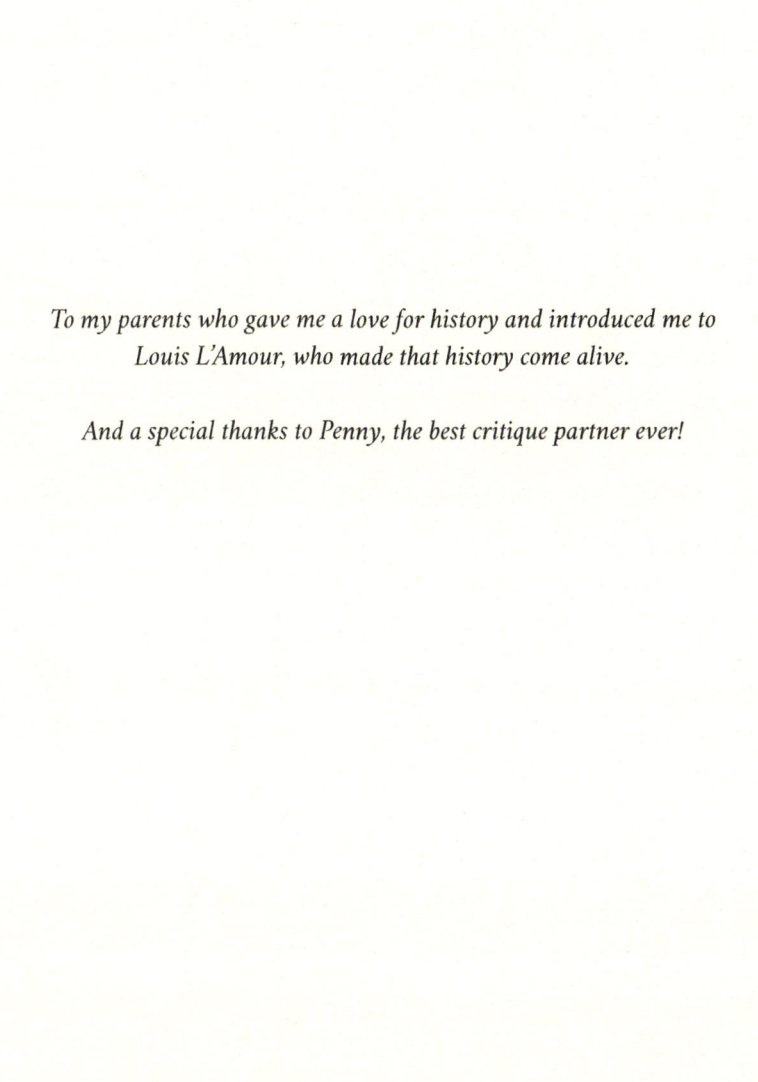

To my parents who gave me a love for history and introduced me to Louis L'Amour, who made that history come alive.

And a special thanks to Penny, the best critique partner ever!

CHAPTER 1

Savannah, Georgia, September 1838

Sophia Deveraux smiled at the beauty of the countryside as she headed back to her family home. The land lay quiet in the fading light of the day. She'd spent the day wandering around the bustling port town of Savannah as she searched for the perfect birthday present for her father. It had been a wonderful day; the first she'd had since her mother's accidental death the previous month. Her father had had an extremely difficult time accepting it, which made her present even more important.

She pulled the exquisite frame from the satchel she'd tucked between the heavy material of her dress and the pommel of the sidesaddle, her thumb tracing the beautiful filigree etching on the black frame. The artisan who'd created the mourning frame of her mother had done a remarkable job. He'd wound her mother's blonde hair in a filigree design that matched the frame and accentuated the yellowing picture of her mother's smiling face.

She had been told enough by her mother, as well as her

mother's closest friends, that it was regrettable Sophia didn't have her mother's refined features and porcelain complexion. With her sun-kissed skin and chestnut hair, she must have taken after a long lost relative on her father's side of the family, although from the few portraits hanging in their front hall, most of them had either blond or red hair.

Tucking the frame back into her satchel for protection, she shrugged off the melancholy stirred up by the memories. Living with her mother had not been easy; she hadn't had a pleasant upbringing. Her mother had always criticized everything she'd done, from education to how she dressed or styled her hair—which was so straight it was always falling out of the coiffure her maid would painstakingly put it in.

Swallowing her sigh, she refused to end such a wonderful day feeling sorry for herself. She was so looking forward to watching her father's reaction when he saw the frame. She was also looking forward to eating the Black Forest cake she'd instructed the cook to make with her father's favorite cherry brandy. Her stomach growled just thinking of sinking her teeth into the moist, cherry-topped chocolate cake.

Several shouts captured her attention as her horse plodded along the newly-bricked lane leading to her family's plantation home. A bright light coming from the front lawn filled the darkening sky, and she could see what looked like a whole regiment of men standing around the large Georgian structure. She pulled the horse to a stop and slowly forced it to back up until they were hidden behind the large live oaks growing over the lane.

From her vantage point, she watched as three of the men marched up the grand marble staircase to the wide front door, which was already standing open. Pale yellow light from the inside lamps poured through the doorway. A tight sensation closed off her throat as fear for her father became a living thing inside of her, trying to claw its way out as she worked to figure out what she should do. She was just one lone female, and there were so many men surrounding her home.

She gripped the reins like a lifeline, desperately trying to make a decision, when it was made for her. Silhouetted in the lamplight stood a familiar figure—the one man she wished she'd never met. Major Adrian Todd presented himself as a gentleman, but after accosting her at a party, she'd learned otherwise and refused the suit her mother had worked tirelessly for.

Her mother all but accused Sophia of purposely turning the major away. That was the final straw in their already rocky relationship. Sophia's entire life had been spent trying to please her mother. She could still hear her mother's icy tone telling her she would always be a disappointment and that she would do whatever it took to remove Sophia from her home.

Sophia patted the horse's neck and wrapped the reins around a thin branch. She crept through the underbrush until she found the well-worn path she'd played along with her old nanny's children, Sally and Tom. She thought back fondly to the fun they'd had fishing and playing in the nearby creek.

Making her way to the back of the house, she crept inside through the slaves' entrance and up the wooden stairs to the back hallway near the dining room. Gently twisting the doorknob, she pushed the door open just a crack so she could see if anyone was inside. The room was dark and quiet. She tiptoed through the room, moving around the chairs and large oak table, using the streams of moonlight as her guide.

Poking her head into the main hall to see if anyone was about, a huge shadow loomed above her. Terror exploded inside her chest and, before she could stop herself, she screamed. Another man instantly appeared, his large, beefy hand reaching for her as he pulled her into the main hall.

"Quit your caterwauling, woman," the man holding her said, each word sharp and pronounced. "Won't do you no good anyway. No one here can help you." He proceeded to shake her hard enough that her head slammed against his massive chest, causing her to bite her tongue. The sudden pain effectively stopped the scream. Pressing her lips together, her tongue throbbed as she clenched her jaws so tightly her teeth ached.

From where she stood, the flickering light of the fireplace in the sitting room across the hall had died down, its still-smoldering embers glowing. The full moon's brightness filtered through the thin curtains that covered the room's two windows. She glanced up, able to see the men only too well, their menacing expressions sending cold shivers down her back.

Thick shadows hung like a heavy curtain behind the two men. A flicker of movement held her gaze. Squinting, she stared at the wall until she made out the indistinct form of a man hidden in the darkness. A painful gasp scraped down her throat when the moon's glow momentarily brightened, and the dark shadows recoiled. The sight of the major's cold, lifeless eyes seared into her mind.

She swallowed her next breath, its sharp trail searing a path down the inside of her chest and constricting it in a tightening vise. The major's slight frame advanced toward her. Without thinking, she tried to scoot back, but her frantic motions were stopped by the immovable arms holding her in place.

Small tingles of dread bit across her chilled skin, quickly turning into larger spikes as waves of malevolence washed over her. Pulling her gaze from his, she struggled. *Where was her father? The servants?*

"Well, my dear, I warned you. Didn't I? I told you I *always* get what I want," his thin, reedy voice taunted as he stopped in front of her, his face only a few inches from hers.

Sophia gathered what little courage she possessed and spit in his face. The major's gloved hand whipped upward and struck her. The sharp *slap* against her cheek echoed through the space. The force of the hit threw her head sideways, and for a few seconds her vision blurred. Pain ripped through her lip, and she tasted the bitter copper flavor of blood. The only sound in the quiet room was her own strangled whimper.

I will not cry. I will not cry. Where is everyone? Someone should have been here by now...

She mentally shook herself, trying to stop the fluttery tremors of terror as its force moved her slight body. She pinched a tiny bit of skin on her thigh, the sharp pain immediately cutting through some of the mind-numbing fear as she tried to figure out a way to escape...but nothing came to mind. She couldn't leave her father.

Major Todd grabbed her by the arms and jerked her away from her captor, pulling her against him. "You will learn better manners when we are married, my dear Ms. Deveraux," he hissed in her ear.

A quick shot of anger replaced some of the fear freezing the blood in her veins. "I will *never* be your wife. I'd rather wallow with pigs!" She pulled as far away from him as his tight grip would allow, which wasn't very far. The cold, abrasive look in his eyes caused her heart to flutter painfully inside her chest. Instinctively, she knew she was in trouble. "You are a commissioned officer—the Army won't let you get away with this," she pleaded. Blinking several times, she forced back the burning tears threatening to spill from her eyes. She refused to let him see just how upset she really was.

"You will pay for your insults, dear Sophia, and you will

wish you'd accepted my proposal. You think to call me a filthy animal? You will soon learn the definition of animal where you're going." He shoved her back into her captor's arms and left the room, his boot heels tapping in a clipped rhythm against the polished floorboards. He stopped in the middle of the hallway and turned his head back to her with a sneer. "Oh, and I *can* and *will* 'get away with it,' as you so succinctly stated. I am an admirable soldier, and have proven my worth time and again. General Scott would never question my honor."

With a quick flip of one finger, he motioned for the soldier holding her to move her forward, placing her at his side. He pinched her trembling chin between his fingers and tilted her head up. "Love is such an honorable notion…is it not?" His tight-lipped grin turned her stomach upside down. "I have convinced Scott we are in love." He tilted her head back, her neck cramping painfully, as his eyes moved over her face. "You would do anything for your father?"

Her eyes widened, and she tried to nod, but his grip on her chin was unrelenting. "Then, my dear, I suggest you do as I tell you. You will display the manners your mother so painstakingly tried to teach you, and come with me quietly and without struggle. Otherwise…" His low chuckle sounded sinister, sending a new burst of fear through her that settled in her stomach like a heavy stone.

She'd never seen evil before, but as she stared into the major's eyes, she knew without a doubt evil stared back at her. She forced her frozen muscles to move, and twisted her body against the tight grip of the soldier who'd taken hold of her again. His fingers dug painfully into her tender skin. As if her efforts were nothing more than the annoying buzz of a fly, the man jerked her into step behind the major. She stumbled along the hall, which led past the grand staircase to the second floor.

Knowing she was running out of time, she planted her feet and pushed her body back into the guard, but still nothing happened. The man was as solid and as immovable as a brick wall. He shoved her forward, and she caught a quick glimpse of the library through the open double-doors. The room was her father's private domain. He would never leave one door open, much less both. When the soldier pushed her forward, she saw her father. His arms and legs had been tied to a chair placed in the center of the room. His face was bloody and swollen, and one hand dangled at an awkward angle. She stared at the bright red splotches of blood on the front of his torn white shirt. He tried to raise his head, holding it up only long enough for their eyes to meet before it fell forward again to rest against his chest.

A pained cry tore through her pinched lips. "Papa!" She struggled to get away. Get to her father. "Why are you doing this?" She screamed at the major.

He turned his head just enough for her to see his profile in the candlelight flickering from the sconces lining the main hall. "Because I can. Your father will soon learn he can't keep from me what's mine. And, my dear, dear Sophia, you are definitely mine."

Shocked and dazed at what was happening to her and her family, she had no strength left to fight and let her captors easily pull her onto the front portico. The numbness spreading over her was a welcome relief.

A loud commotion pulled her gaze toward the end of the street where a group of soldiers on horseback were shouting and laughing. She saw rather than heard the harsh *crack* of their whips and the slaves' answering screams. It was simply too much for her to comprehend, and she welcomed the darkness with open arms.

CHAPTER 2

Fort Wool, New Echota, Georgia, October 1838

Hunger pains gnawed at the inside of Sophia's shrunken stomach. She moved and smelled her own sweaty body. She stank…plus her dirt wore dirt, which made it worse. She gazed across the crowded courtyard. Bleakness and loss surrounded her in her prison. Having grown up in a beautiful plantation home surrounded by the finest things money could buy, she'd never really given much thought to her surroundings. She'd always been more concerned about the people inside her home and how they were living. *This place, though? This place she hated.*

She stared into the blank faces of the starving and abused Cherokee families as they inched their way around the too-small enclosure. So many whys pushed through her mind until she thought she would go crazy. She still couldn't quite fathom the reasons behind Major Todd's actions of placing her there. After fainting the horrible night of her abduction, Sophia didn't remember how she got here. She woke up to find herself in the fort surrounded by Cherokee Indians.

Her thoughts turned back to the major and asked herself the same questions for the thousandth time. Why would a decorated soldier care what she thought about him? And why lock her up with the Cherokee? None of it made any sense to her.

Her gaze scanned the prisoners inside the fort's interior, their worn clothing and emaciated bodies. These kind and loving people treated her better than her own kind had. Even during this terrible time, their numbers diminishing daily as more and more died from the deplorable conditions and lack of food, they continued to care for her, in spite of the fact that she was white. Especially Martin. He'd taken care of her almost from the moment she'd opened her eyes and found she was a prisoner. Over the last few weeks, the elderly Indian had taken a special interest in her, acting more like a grandfather than a friend...at least how she imagined a grandfather would be if she'd ever known one. Everything she now knew about the Cherokee was so very wrong from what she'd been taught.

Sophia turned away from the gruesome sight of the growing mound of bodies in the corner of the fort. It was a constant reminder of just how dire their situation was. As she did several times each day, she rose on her tiptoes and searched through the crowd of listless bodies until she found Martin sitting against the far wall.

Carefully making her way across the courtyard, she pushed through the last line of people and stood in front of Martin. With no care for the tiny ants scurrying through the loose sand—or how unladylike she'd become—Sophia dropped down beside him and crossed her legs as the Indians did, which was a surprisingly comfortable position.

"Martin? Why are we still here? Why are we held here like prisoners?" Her words came out clipped, but Martin didn't seem to notice.

"One of the more friendly guards told me our departure was changed to avoid the hot weather," he answered in his usual calm manner. "I did not want you to worry more, so I said nothing."

Sophia sighed. "I was afraid of that. You've been too cheerful." She tucked her arm through his and wrapped her fingers around his balled fist. "I'm not a little child. I can handle more than you think." A smile tugged at one side of her mouth, and she bumped him gently with her shoulder. "I just wish I could understand why this is happening to your people."

Martin's lip curled in disgust, and his eyes narrowed into small slits on his weathered face. "The white man is not interested in the care of our land but in its riches—specifically, gold." Sophia's eyebrows furrowed together as several more questions popped into her head, but she pressed her lips together, biting her tongue in order to keep silent. "Our homeland is fertile, and we were able to grow many kinds of crops. Over the years, white men crossed our lands. They found gems, gold, and silver and wanted it for themselves. The Choctaw and several other tribes have already resettled out west, including my best friend, Strong Eagle, and his family. I miss them."

She watched his gaze shift from hers to the empty space over her shoulder, and squeezed his hand. She didn't want to press him for more, but she needed to have answers. "So, everyone here will be moved west as well? How far west will they take us?"

He didn't answer. Several minutes passed in silence. His gaze was empty as he continued to stare over her shoulder.

"My wife and I were brought here with everyone else."

She frowned in confusion. "Your wife?" At times since her arrival, he'd worn his sorrow like a cloak, but she hadn't known him well enough to ask at first. Then as time passed, she'd never found a good time to ask him what weighed so heavy on his heart. Turning her head slightly, she followed the direction of his gaze, which was focused on the mound of bodies in the corner behind her. She closed her eyes for a moment, wishing she could take back the question. His sadness was palpable. She threaded her fingers through his. "Martin, I am so very sorry."

He shrugged, his gaze dropping to their clasped hands. "She was sick for a while. We knew it was only a matter of time. I just wish it hadn't been here."

She wanted to comfort him, to at least say something to ease his obvious heartache, but she couldn't find the words. She'd never faced so much loss before and wasn't sure how to help herself much less help Martin. The only real family she'd ever known was her mother and father, but it had been her old nanny and her nanny's two children who'd taught her what the bond of family should be.

Martin sadly patted her knee. She wasn't sure whether he was trying to comfort her or himself. "The *Ani'Yun'wiya* have lived and cared for these lands many lifetimes—it is with heavy hearts that we leave our homes.

From her first day in the godforsaken fort, she had witnessed the Cherokees' abuse at the hands of the soldiers. The generous people had been starved and beaten. She gazed at the fort's inhabitants, clumped together in family groups. Her chest tightened at the pathetic sight. She tamped down an intense, unfamiliar flood of anger. "Surely the government doesn't want the Cherokee treated like this?" she whispered.

Martin smiled. If the tiny lift of his lips could be called a smile. "No, little one. General Scott is a good man. I was there when he gave the orders for all of us to receive food and blankets. Because so many here have died, he also commanded that the soldiers treat us better…but these orders are not obeyed."

"And the other? What was the word you used…ani-something."

His smile widened. "*Ani'Yun'wiya*. That is who we are." He raised his free hand with a quick motion toward the people surrounding them. "It is what we call ourselves. The name was given to us by the ancient Cherokee who passed before. *Ani'Yun'wiya* means the Principal People."

"Why do you talk differently than the other Cherokee? Did you go to school? And why don't you go by your Indian name?"

"You have many questions," he grunted, but Sophia caught the approval glistening in his clear eyes. "Martin is my only name. As more white families settled these lands, my grandfather believed we would need white names, so trading between our people would be easier and we wouldn't seem too different. My father had two names, Cherokee and white. By the time I was born, he never used his Cherokee name, and I was only Martin."

Sophia's admiration for the old Indian grew as she listened. In spite of everything his people had been through, the Cherokee spirit remained strong. Even as death hovered, waiting for its next victim, Sophia observed their loving regard for one another—and not just the individual families. They seemed more like one huge family.

"I attended William and Mary, the white man's college in Virginia," Martin said, pushing out his thin chest with pride. "My father insisted. He was a smart man, my father. He watched as the white settlements grew larger. He told me I must become an important person—that the Cherokee would need important people to survive." Sophia watched his bony shoulders wilt. "I don't feel so important now."

"I know it isn't much, but you are very important to me."

She placed her small hand over Martin's skeletal arm and squeezed. Her tentative smile disappeared as his bushy gray brows drew together and his gaze hardened.

"Martin?"

He gently patted her arm and forced his stiff old body into a stand. "I will return shortly."

Sophia turned and watched as he made his way toward the front of the fort. He stopped beside one of the fort's tall log doors and crossed his arms over his thin chest. She leaned to one side to see what Martin was doing and saw him talking to a very handsome man. Her eyebrows rose as she peered closer. The younger man's face could have been chiseled from stone. He had high cheekbones and a perfect nose, and his skin was dark like the Cherokees. Even though she was too far away to be certain, his eyes looked black.

As if he knew he was being studied, his dark gaze quickly moved around the enclosure, finally landing on her. Even with the distance between them, her stomach knotted, and a small kernel of fear balled in her stomach. His gaze seemed to pierce her soul. The hairs on her arms and neck rose the longer he stared…his piercing gaze made her feel as if she were being stalked by a predator. Forcing herself to look away, she decided she wasn't that curious about who he was after all. She couldn't help herself, however—two seconds later, she was studying him again. He wore dark gray wool trousers and a light gray shirt covered by a soft-looking brown leather coat. The clothing almost fooled her, but she knew he was an Indian. If so, how was he able to ride around the countryside without being locked up?

A sharp yell pulled her attention away from his handsome face to a group of boys who were hitting a small rock back and forth between them with a stick. The hair on her arms and back of her neck rose, and she had the eerie sensation of being watched. She slowly scanned the stockade, trying to find whoever was staring at her. She finally noticed a uniformed soldier standing under the shaded overhang of a small shed several feet away, but she couldn't see his face until he stepped out into the early morning sunshine. She sucked in a breath, holding it until her lungs burned. It was Major Todd. His hooded gaze followed her every move.

Uncomfortable and not wanting to talk to the major or draw any attention to herself, Sophia stood, her palms nervously trying to smooth the tattered material of her skirt. It had been a gift from one of the women who'd taken pity on her the night she'd arrived wearing her dirty nightgown. She despised the ill-fitting and scratchy garment but refused to complain. It was much more proper than the nightgown.

She turned to walk toward Martin and the handsome stranger, but before she could finish the forward motion of her step, a hand wrapped around her upper arm and squeezed. She fell backward and hit something hard enough to knock the air from her lungs.

"You try my patience, dear Sophia." Major Todd said in a low growl. She tried to pull away, but his grip was too tight. All she could do was try to keep upright as he shoved her through several small groups of Indians who backed away from them, their eyes wide with fear.

"Did you think I wouldn't notice?" he asked then pushed her into the small shed where he'd watched her from a few moments earlier. Frantically, her gaze darted around the room, trying to find some way to protect herself...so she wasn't prepared when he wrapped his hand tightly around her throat and shoved her against the hard wooden logs of the room's wall. Something jabbed into her back, but the sharp pain was nothing compared to the constricted burn spreading through her chest as she tried to breathe.

Clawing at his short, stubby fingers, she gasped in minute amounts of air. After several seconds, she wheezed, "What…

what...did I...do?" The major ignored her struggle. Dark spots floated in her dimming field of vision as her air-deprived lungs burned.

"You are spending too much time with that *Indian*," he spat. "Have you slept with him yet?" The back of his other hand slammed across her face. "Whore," he spit out, then slapped her again, whipping her head in the other direction sideways. His grip around her throat loosened, and she gulped air in.

The stench of his foul breath as it blasted across her face made her want to retch. She swallowed furiously, trying to control the upward flow of bile in the back of her throat. Tears of pain and frustration filled her eyes, but she refused to let a single one fall. His eyes narrowed, and a strangled sob caught in her tight throat as fear raced through her battered body. "Martin is like a grandfather to me. Nothing more." She choked out the words. Her body felt like it was on fire, but strangely, her face felt numb.

A small tic began in his right eye and he took one slow step back, his hand dropping to his side. She pulled herself upright and eased away from whatever had been digging into her shoulder blades. With each deep, calming breath, the tremors faded from her exhausted muscles, and her body stilled. No matter how much this man tormented her, she refused to appear weak, or let him know how much his actions and words affected her.

"He might have lived in a regular house and worn our clothing, but he's still a filthy Indian. Your mother worked too hard to make you into a lady—a *white* lady, I might add. Do not disappoint me again. Next time, I will not be as forgiving, and you will be treated like the rest of these savages."

She let her gaze follow him as he clomped across the room. He might as well have been speaking in a foreign language, because she hadn't understood what he'd just said. She gently massaged her tender neck, her thoughts chaotic as she tried to figure out the major's insinuation—both about the 'white lady' as well as her treatment. She wasn't treated any differently than the Cherokee, and the other remark made no sense to her at all.

The slight squeak of the hinges as the major opened the door pulled her out of her thoughts, and her breath caught in her chest when he stopped. Thankfully, he didn't turn but simply pinned her with his dark gaze as he glared at her over his shoulder. The slimy smirk on his face made her empty stomach roil. "You will learn to do as you're told. I was promised your cooperation."

After the door slammed shut behind him, her shaking returned, now more with anger than fear. "How dare he?" she whispered. "He is delusional if he thinks I will ever be his wife." She might be young and alone, but she wasn't without her own gifts. A lifetime of dodging her mother's foul temper and underhanded slights had given her strength. From somewhere deep inside her, she drew on that power. Without a doubt, she knew she would be able to handle whatever the major threw at her.

Edging around the door, she hung her head and picked her way through the crowd, trying to remain invisible to curious gazes. Gingerly, she lowered her sore body to the ground at the base of the far wall, one side of her frame pressed against the rough wood, and tucked her feet underneath her. With her head against the wall, she closed her eyes. The voices around her faded into the background as exhaustion claimed her.

"Oh, Lord. What happened to you?"

The young male voice startled her awake. Her eyes flew open and she glanced up, instinctively scooting away from the young man despite the soreness in her muscles. When her sluggish mind realized it wasn't Major Todd, but another young soldier she'd occasionally seen standing guard, she relaxed. His wide-eyed, sky blue gaze and open mouth steadied the choking panic writhing in her gut. He had the appearance of a gangly youth, more arms and legs than bulk. He was very cute, though, and in about ten years would mature into a handsome man.

"I ran into a small problem." She grimaced. Her slender fingers hovered over her cheek, then dropped into her lap. "Is it very noticeable?"

The young soldier stared down at her swollen face. He shook his head, the sunlight catching pale red highlights in his brown hair, but she could see the uncertainty in his gaze. "Not too much." He squatted and handed her a bundle loosely held in his grip. When she took the wad of material from him, he sat back on his heels. "Who did this?" He jerked his head toward the large group at his back, his gaze locked with hers. "The Cherokee are good people. They wouldn't have done this." Realization dawned and his eyes widened. "It was a soldier, wasn't it?"

Sophia didn't answer. Carefully, she unwrapped the dirty blanket and stared into the age-cracked porcelain face of the antique doll her father had given her as a child. Closing her eyes, she took a deep breath. She hadn't told anyone about her problems with the major, or how she'd ended up at the fort; for whatever reason, she surprised herself and told the young soldier everything.

After a short silence, another voice joined their quiet conversation. "Child, why did you not tell me?" Martin leaned forward and tipped her face up with the tips of his fingers. Sadness filled his eyes as he stared at her swollen cheek. "We take care of each other. That is what family does. You are a part of the Cherokee family now. Of my family."

So many feelings flooded through her, filling her heart

until her chest ached. She clutched the doll to her chest, drawing strength from her father's gift. Her heart felt shredded. She wanted nothing more than for her father to show up at the gate to take her home—but now that she had Martin, she knew she couldn't leave him either.

Looking up, she met the older Indian's worried gaze. "I'm all right. At least I will be." She nestled the doll in her lap and willed her jittery stomach to calm down. "My old nanny's daughter, Sally, told me the major was a bad man. She used to say, 'He has devil eyes, Miss Sophia. I seen the fires a-burnin' in them. Devil eyes.'" She blinked back the threatening rush of tears. "Sally was right, you know," she whispered.

"Excuse me. Sir?" The young soldier motioned for Martin to follow him a few feet away.

Sophia watched Martin quickly glance at the doll draped across her lap, but he didn't ask about it, and she was simply too tired to explain. Crossing his arms over his chest, he turned to face the young man.

"Name's Bryan, sir. Bryan MacConnell." His voice lowered, and she had to focus to hear his words over the background noises filtering in. "I haven't been here long, but I've seen how you take care of her, sir. Major Todd ordered me to give her the doll, but when I saw what he'd done to her, I couldn't give her his message."

"What's the message? I will tell Sophia when she's feeling better."

Bryan shuffled from one foot to the other. "I don't rightly understand it, but he wanted her to know her father wouldn't be comin' for her. Said he was restin' with her mother."

Sophia heard a cry filled with so much pain it brought tears to her eyes, and was startled to realize the cry had come from her. Unaware of the stream of tears staining her face as she gasped for air, she felt arms wrap around her trembling shoulders. She cried until she couldn't cry anymore, then gently pulled away from Martin with a loud hiccup. She wiped her face with the backs of her hands. "Thank you," she whispered. "When I heard what Bryan said…" She clenched her jaws together, willing away the overwhelming grief threatening to erupt all over again.

"Miss Sophia, I don't understand. Your parents are together. That's good, isn't it?" Bryan's face pulled into a lopsided frown.

She moved her head slowly from side to side as more tears again trickled down her face. She drew in a shaky breath. "No, that's not good. My mother's dead." She turned her soggy gaze to Martin. "The major killed my father." Sorrow consumed her body, squeezing and crushing her chest. She bit the tender flesh on the inside of her cheeks, the momentary sting of pain giving her a brief reprieve.

From somewhere deep inside her, a small spark stuttered, then roared to life. She pushed her shoulders back and sat up straighter. Crying and feeling sorry for herself would do her no good. She let loose the strong will and determination that had cost her a close relationship with a mother. Sophia was going to use the very thing that had made her life miserable as a weapon against the major.

Martin's joints popped and creaked as he lowered himself to sit beside her. Finally, after a few grunts and moans while crossing his legs, he managed to get comfortable. Not wanting any more questions, she changed the subject. "Martin, who were you talking to earlier?"

His eyes sparkled. "He is the son of my best friend, Strong Eagle. They were relocated several years ago with the rest of their tribe to the lands promised by President Jackson. Strong Eagle's son is named Clay."

"Only Clay?" she prodded.

"When he joined the Lighthorse, Clay took the last name of Jefferson after the third president. He believed taking a last name like everyone else would allow the White law to respect him more if he seemed more like them.

"Clay asked me questions about the relocation—and our treatment here. The Cherokee Council wants to try to stop the move."

"What is the Lighthorse?" Sophia asked, trying to convince herself she was more interested in the Indian history than Martin's handsome friend.

"It is a group of appointed warriors who uphold Choctaw laws—an honorable profession among the tribe."

"Does Clay also have an Indian name?"

Martin nodded. "Nighthawk."

"Nighthawk," she quietly repeated. She knew nothing about Indian names, but his sounded strong. Clay's handsome face shadowed her thoughts as her tired mind replayed the day's events. She wanted to know more about Clay. How did he know Martin was here, and why would the council have sent him? Clay was also an Indian, so how was he able to avoid recapture? A small kernel of hope began to form. She wanted to see Clay Jefferson again. Maybe she would even muster enough nerve to talk to him, too.

CHAPTER 3

*D*irty and tired, Clay left Fort Wool and rode into the small town of New Echota, Georgia. He'd pushed hard to get the information he'd gathered from the Indian Territory where his Choctaw tribe had been relocated to the leader of the Cherokee, Chief Ross. Clay needed a bath and sleep, but still had ten more hours of riding before he would arrive at the Cherokees' newest council house in Red Clay, Tennessee.

The last time he'd been in New Echota, people had bustled along the carriage-rutted street, shopping and visiting with one another. The town had been brimming with life and laughter. Now, however, it resembled a ghost town. On the far edge of town, he stopped at a small farm owned by a long-time friend of Martin's to trade his tired horse for a fresh one. After transferring his gear to a well-muscled bay, he rode north. The small, picturesque town disappeared behind him. The moment he hit the trail, he urged the horse into a gallop. He would have to alternate with occasional walks, but he and his new four-legged companion had forty-one miles to go and no time left.

Seven hours later, Clay rode up to the skeletal council house where several men hovered around the lodge's central fire pit. Evidently there hadn't been time to build anything more than the four corner posts before putting the building to use. He slid off the bay and wiped down the sweaty horse as best he could, then led the tired animal over to a group of horses already drinking in a shallow creek.

Stretching his muscles, sore from long hours spent in the saddle, he made his way across a carpet of browning grass dotted with spots of sandy soil and tall, spindly weeds leading to the council house. Just inside the entrance, three men stepped into his path. Dark clouds floated over the moon's bright glow and distorted their features, casting a macabre look to their angry expressions. Clay watched the emotions twist and mold his long-time friends' faces, and wondered what had just transpired within the small circle of elders to erase their usual smiles.

Clay nodded toward each man. "Seth, Thomas, Michael. What has happened?" Knowing they wouldn't let him through until they were good and ready, Clay propped one foot against a large rock near the house's foundation and rested his elbow across his knee as he waited for their answer.

Seth, the tallest and oldest of the three brothers, stepped forward. "The council members have agreed to try one more time, asking the President to overturn the removal act and stop the final march." With a flick of one wrist, Seth motioned toward the group of men inside who were talking heatedly amongst themselves. "The soldiers are foolish! Our people should be gathering food and necessary items for survival. Only the white man would be stupid enough to travel during the worst of winter."

"*A-se-hi.*" Seth's two brothers shouted *yes* in Cherokee.

Clay straightened and crossed his arms over his chest,

willing away the tension from his tight muscles. "I, too, wish to stop the removal, but I'm afraid it's too late for that. Too many in the stockades die daily. Like you, I also agree something must be done now, but we need to petition President Jackson to provide food and appropriate clothing—everything the Cherokee will need to survive such a dangerous journey."

He took a step forward and casually placed a hand on Seth's shoulder for a moment, then continued into the open structure. The day's light had faded, but the orange firelight flickered over the dour look on John Ross's face. Clay watched as the chief's jaws clenched and unclenched in frustration.

Clay adopted the chief's rigid stance a few feet away from the other council members. "Has a decision been made?"

Ross's lips thinned, almost disappearing as his mouth tightened, and shook his head. With a quick jerk of his head, he indicated for Clay to follow as he walked toward the six men, still debating amongst themselves in low, angry voices. The moment Ross stepped up to their tight circle, all talking stopped. Each man faced him respectfully, their faces blank. Ross took a firm hold of Clay's upper arm and pulled him forward into the circle.

"This is the man I told you about. Clay Jefferson. His Choctaw tribe was the first moved to the Indian Territory. During their march, many Indians died, including his own family."

Clay watched the variety of minute changes crossing each man's face, from narrowed eyes to tightened lips to open anxiety. "I asked Clay to gather as much information as he could so that I could present our case one last time to President Jackson." Chief Ross turned his hard gaze to Clay.

Clay nodded. "The Choctaw were divided into three groups, with the first group transported in November 1831.

General Gibson planned and routed our journeys but met with horrible results. The guides did not know the way, we had no transports—either by land or river—and we were never given enough supplies for food or warmth. These were just a few of the problems. Gibson does not care about the Indians, no matter the tribe. Most of the citizens living in Vicksburg had already died from a white-man disease called cholera. The general took us there anyway."

He paused, taking several deep breaths, pushing back the overwhelming grief and sense of helplessness that always surfaced when he was forced to relive the agonizing memories. "My mother, father, and younger sister almost made it to our new home, but were murdered when we left the river." He met each council member's gaze and noted the sadness greeting him in return. "More than two thousand Choctaw died before they arrived in Indian Territory."

Clay shifted his feet. "The Elders from several forts gave me information about the ongoing Cherokees' imprisonment. Too many are packed into the central outdoor area of each fort—unable to move around, the sick and the young die by the hour. Many young warriors have been beaten to death for no reason. There is a mountain of unburied bodies at each fort." Clay clenched his fists, but wouldn't allow himself any other reaction in front of these men. "Chief Ross is right. The Cherokee do not want the same fate as the Choctaw. If the Cherokee are forced to march as my tribe was, many more will die when winter arrives."

His job done, he turned on his heel to leave without waiting for a response. Ross clapped him on his shoulder in passing but didn't say anything. Clay walked from the building, chased by the sounds of arguing as Ross tried to reason with the stubborn men. He didn't like it, but he understood. The Choctaw leaders had responded in much the same way. One thing he knew for certain; the Cherokee could rely on the consistency of the United States government in their dismal treatment of the Indians—to the detriment of the tribes.

He grabbed the reins and mounted the bay, setting a slow pace as he left Tennessee to begin the long trip home. His thoughts wandered back to the beautiful girl he'd seen back at Fort Wool. Her haunted eyes had pulled at something deep inside him—a feeling he thought he'd lost with the death of his family. The longer she'd held his gaze, the more he'd wanted to stay.

When the bay stumbled over the rocky ground, he realized the slow pace wasn't enough. With the horse too exhausted to continue, he found a good place to stop and made camp for the night.

For about a week, he'd looked forward to eating meat again, having finished the remainder of his aunt's venison. He'd eaten the last of his supply of hickory nuts and berries, so he was more than starving. After several failed attempts, he'd managed to kill one small bird with his blowgun. The heat from his small fire felt good in the crisp night air as he turned the skewered quail held just above the flames in a spit made from twigs. His mouth watered from the scent of the roasting meat.

When the bird was cooked, he ate every morsel from the tiny bones. He added a few more logs to the fire, stirring the ashes underneath, the growing flames rising toward the heavens. He lay back on the hard ground and propped his head against his saddle, listening to crickets chirping back and forth. His thoughts returned to the council. Watching the thin film of smoke curling into the night sky, a bad feeling churned in his gut. He dreaded the approaching turmoil between the soldiers and the Cherokee. The only somewhat comforting thought was that he could now continue searching for the men who'd killed his family. His eyes closed and the tightness in his muscles slowly loosened.

A faint crack sounded to his left. Before he could move, the cold bite of a knife blade pressed against the tender skin of his throat, making it hard to swallow. The smell of sour sweat and tobacco wafted over him, and his stomach clenched uncomfortably. The only visible part of his attacker was a tattered, dark blue sleeve. A section of the frayed gold trim that had at one time adorned the coat now dangled where the stitches had been pulled out. When whoever held him moved to get a better grip on him, Clay caught a quick glimpse of a filthy, light blue pant leg and muddy boots. He couldn't help but wonder whether the soldier ever bathed.

"What...?" Clay started to ask but bit back the words when a fiery burn moved across his neck as the soldier pushed the knife deeper into his skin.

"You gonna be sorry, injun. Should've turned yerself in with them others," the soldier groused. He pulled Clay's upper body off the ground as he moved backward. The man's harsh tug pushed his chin higher and made breathing difficult.

"Hey, Joel! Git over here an' help me tie 'im up!"

"I'm a comin'!" a higher-pitched voice yelled behind them.

"I'm a captain in the Choctaw Lighthorse—a lawman," Clay explained, waiting to see what they were going to do. From the look of the soldiers, they weren't going to believe him, much less let him go. The moment he was bound, any hope for freedom would be gone. Joel—who looked to be about twenty, and was just as grimy as the other man—squatted at his feet with a rope in his hands and a sneer on his face. Before the soldier could tie his ankles together, Clay kicked and struck Joel's arm. He used the distraction of the kid's high-pitched squeal to twist out of the first soldier's hold. Unfortunately, when he tried rolling to his feet, the larger man got in a good kick and knocked him back to the ground. When Clay's head hit a rock, he felt the skin on his cheekbone split open.

When both soldiers kicked his midsection and back at the same time, his unplanned escape escalated into a fight for his life. Each ensuing blow landed with sharp, burning stabs of pain until he lay immobile, unable to move. His arms were painfully jerked behind him and tied together, blending a final burst of pain with all the rest and pulling him down into a merciful, unfeeling void.

CHAPTER 4

Near Nashville, Tennessee

"It's time to move out. The Colonel is already angry—said we should've been marching an hour ago." Bryan's voice held a note of apology as he gave them the news.

Sophia shivered from the icy chill covering her skin as well as his words. She stared out at the sleeping landscape, now covered in a thick white glaze. Naked shrubs and skeletal trees hovered on both sides of the thin dirt trail, but gave little shelter against the harsh sting of the bitter December wind. The stark surroundings seemed quite fitting for what she and the Cherokee had already experienced since leaving Fort Wool one week ago. She couldn't help but wonder if the government had known the severity of this year's winter conditions, would they have provided more supplies? Did they even care what happened to any of them?

Walking behind the rickety wagon, she worried over the worsening of Martin's already fragile condition. He'd come down with a high fever the day after they'd left the relative safety of the fort. To make matters worse, the Cherokee medicine man had died, leaving no one to take his place. She watched the man she'd come to think of as her grandfather, and wished for the hundredth time that he could see a doctor. Unable to sit and do nothing, she'd asked the healer's widow to try to perform a healing in desperation. It had appeared to be working until several days ago, when Martin's fever had risen once more.

He now sat in the corner of the wagon, huddled in his thin gray blanket as the wind buffeted him from all sides. Having a canvas over the wagons would have been preferable, but only the military wagons were covered. Deep lines etched into his face made him seem older than his almost sixty years. What scared her most was the emptiness she saw in his dark brown eyes. That reassuring light she'd begun to count on was gone.

Ignoring her frozen muscles, she stepped up her pace. Half walking, half running, she caught the side of the wagon with her hand, using it to propel her forward without falling. "Martin, are you okay?" Her brow furrowed. "Martin?" she asked a little louder.

Martin's head rose until he met her worried gaze. "I am fine, Granddaughter. Just tired."

"Are you warm enough? I can give you my blanket if you'd like."

The corners of his dry lips tried to rise, but their upward movement stalled. He shook his head. "No, I am fine. You need the warmth." He placed his hand over hers, which still gripped the wagon's side. "Stop worrying. You will grow gray hairs."

It was the first lighthearted comment he'd made since leaving New Echota. A surge of emotion poured through her. She wasn't sure if it was relief or happiness—but either way, it gave her hope.

Exhaustion beat at her the longer she walked. Since leaving the fort, they'd walked from sun-up to sun-down, day after day, no matter the weather. The soldiers prodded them along like a herd of cattle. She wasn't about to complain, though, especially when so many of the captives had no blankets or shoes.

Every morning she woke up to discover more people had died—young children and the elderly, their bodies too fragile to fight off the night's freezing temperatures. That morning had been particularly hard; while getting Martin's morning rations, she'd stumbled over an old grandmother and her grandson, frozen to death in each other's grip under their ice-covered blanket. And it was only December. How would they fare in late January and February, when the conditions were bound to worsen?

Shaking her head to clear the memory, she glanced up to find that Bryan had returned. The soldier stood a few feet away, a blanket draped over one arm. She breathed out a sad little sigh and dropped her gaze back to where her hands lay clasped together in her lap.

"What's wrong, Miss Sophia?" Bryan asked.

Remembering the two bodies, her eyes glazed over with unshed tears. She blinked them away, amazed she had any tears left. So many had died. "I wish there was something more I could do for them."

Bryan walked next to her and laid the blanket over her shoulders. "You can't save everyone, Miss Sophia. They died together. Nothin' can hurt 'em anymore."

She sighed. "I know you're right." She met his gaze, ignoring the tears blurring her vision. "He was only four," she whispered brokenly. "He had his whole life ahead of him."

"He's happy now, playin' and laughin' up in God's lands." Bryan cleared his throat, but she still heard the depth of his emotion. He wrapped his hand around hers and gave her numb fingers a small squeeze. He glanced into the wagon. "Is Martin feeling better this morning?"

Her gaze traveled over the group. Threadbare blankets draped over the hunched figures as they marched, and she forced her stiff muscles to keep moving alongside them. "He seems to be in better spirits, but whether or not he feels better, I'm not sure. He won't tell me."

Their numbers had been decreasing daily. She didn't want to think of the lifeless bodies left lying where they'd died. She knew that the Cherokee believed that without a proper burial, their souls couldn't follow the path to their Great Spirit. So every chance she had, she'd been helping the older children cover the corpses with anything they could easily pick up. She'd lived, suffered, and cried alongside these people. Her life back in Savannah seemed such a long time ago…

She glanced down at the scrapes and cuts covering her palms, then tightened her hands into fists. "I *have* made a difference," she whispered to herself. She let out a slow breath and forced her mind back to the present, but was unable to stop the persistent questions pushing through her worn-out mind. *Will we make it? What will happen when we get to wherever they're taking us? How many more of us are going to die?*

THEY'D FINALLY MADE it to Kentucky after living in makeshift camps for two weeks near the town of Nashville. Martin still hadn't fully recovered from his illness and had had somewhat of a morose disposition ever since. Nothing she said or did helped, and she was out of ideas.

Frustrated and grumpy herself, Sophia plodded alongside the wagon and watched the animated discussion playing out between Martin and Bryan. The current argument had returned a spark of life to the old man's eyes, but his tight lips and scowl sent a frisson of dread skittering through her.

She listened to him grumble and growl for almost an hour after Bryan had ridden away, and she couldn't take it anymore. "Oh, for heaven's sake! What has you in such a state? What did Bryan tell you?"

Martin grumbled a few more times then took a deep breath, which ended in a dry, hacking cough. "The man who had been leading us to the new lands was called back to Washington. It seems General Scott appointed Major Todd to lead us the rest of the way." He turned a knowing gaze to her face. "If you must know, I'm scared for you, *Ulisi ageyutsa*, Granddaughter. I fear for your safety. I know he wasn't good to you, and Bryan told me more—of the man's cruelty, both to animals and to his men. And especially to the Cherokee."

She sighed. "I guess somewhere deep inside me, I knew I wouldn't be able to escape him."

Eventually, they stopped for the night. Sophia spread out their blankets underneath the wagon bed and helped Martin crawl underneath. As they lay there, silence covered them like a shroud, broken only by the clopping of the soldiers' horses as they did their nighttime rounds and an occasional creak from the wagons that housed the people fortunate enough to sleep inside them. Weeks ago, she and Martin had agreed to let as many of the children who could fit sleep in theirs.

She stared at the tent of blankets a few of the soldiers had tied onto poles to keep the snow off while they slept, wishing there were enough to cover everyone. Maybe fewer people would die if there were. Her mind wouldn't slow down, however; sleep remained elusive. She focused instead on what she could do to stop Major Todd from carrying out whatever he had planned...and she knew without a shred of doubt that he was definitely up to something.

A prickling sensation started at the base of her neck and inched its way over her body. She sat up and glanced around. Other than sleeping Indians, there was no one there. She couldn't even see the normally ever-present soldiers as they walked the perimeter of the camp.

She hugged her waist and tried to concentrate on three small rocks lying next to her moccasins. She'd felt the same sensation since arriving at Nashville. It was an uneasy presence, as if someone watched her. Unseen eyes burned a trail along her body, making her feel exposed. Dirty. A hard shiver shook her and caught Martin's perceptive gaze.

The wonderful man had attached himself to her heart. The last thing she wanted was for him to worry about her more than he already did. She forced the corners of her mouth to turn upward. "Only a shiver. I think the weather is getting colder, if that's possible."

He nodded. "Very possible, unfortunately." He pointed to the darkening skyline and the thick layer of billowing clouds. "The sky grows heavy. We are in for another bad storm." She watched his eyes lose focus, glazing over as his thoughts turned inward. "I miss her, you know. My Klara." A wry grin split his face. "Especially at times like this. She had the warmest feet."

Sophia slipped her hand into his large one; it was gnarled and rough from age and hard work, but his grip was still strong. In the evening's waning light, her unfashionable olive complexion looked only a few shades lighter than the rich café au lait of his.

A bubbly fullness burst inside her as she finally allowed herself to think of her father. "I miss my family also. Well, my father, anyway. He was a ship's captain, and when he was home, life was magic. He was a large, fun-loving man. I also miss Mamma Lou and Sally. They took care of me."

"And what about your mother?"

Sophia shook her head ruefully. "We didn't get along very well."

Martin squeezed her hand in understanding, then let it drop back into her lap. He brushed the light layer of snow from his blanket, as if needing to do something with his hands. "Tell me about Sally and Mamma Lou."

A rich chuckle slipped through her constricted throat. "Sally is younger than me by four years and is my best friend, although I'm supposed to tell people she's my maid. Mamma Lou is her mother, and my old nanny. Truthfully, she was a mother to me, too. I hope they are both safe."

Martin cupped her chin, and with a gentle brush of his thumb across her cheek, wiped away the tears. "I won't tell you they are, but I will keep that same hope in my heart as well. As my wise father used to tell me, 'Know your enemy, son. Keep them close.' So tell me, how did Major Todd come into your life?"

Sophia couldn't stop the twisting of her features as her eyebrows bunched together, and her lips curled in disgust. "Unfortunately, that was my doing. I disobeyed my parents' decision about not allowing me to attend a soiree that the major was hosting." She stretched the muscles in her face, forcing them to relax, and took a deep, cleansing breath as the memories from that long-ago night resurfaced. "The major asked me to walk with him, said he needed some air. I thought he was so dignified, and being naïve, I allowed him to lead me outside to a small side garden. Before I knew what was happening, his hands were everywhere. No matter how many times I shoved them away, they returned, pawing at me. When I saw Sally sneak up behind him and bash him over the head with a small garden statue, I'd never been more thankful that she'd disobeyed my instructions. I'd told her to stay home. Instead, she knocked him silly enough to give us enough time to get away."

Martin nodded. "Then what happened?"

Sophia smiled. "When we got home, Mamma Lou was waiting up for us. We both got a good tongue-lashing. Mamma Lou said that no matter how old I got, she would put me back on the straight and narrow if she felt I needed it.

"A week later, I went downstairs for a late breakfast. Instead of food, I found the major with my mother. The major lied to her, convincing her that everything had been my fault, but he was willing to do right by me...as long as I had a proper dowry, of course. My mother practically threw me into his outstretched arms. She couldn't agree fast enough."

"And your father? Did he also agree to this plan?"

She shook her head. "No. Thankfully later that day, my father arrived home from his latest sea voyage and convinced her he would make everything right again. Or so I thought. I had just retired to my room when I heard the commotion downstairs. Mamma Lou sent Sallie upstairs to stay with me until the sheriff left. Papa said the doctor believed Mama must have slipped and broken her neck. The strangest thing was where the accident happened. She never went into that room. Never.

"The rest of the story, you already know." She pulled the old doll from the folds of her blanket. In the fading light, her childhood toy looked terrible. The tiny pink dress was torn in several places, and somewhere along the trail she'd lost a shoe. Sophia pulled her own tattered dress over her legs, which were tucked up against her chest, and leaned against the inside of the back wheel. She rested her chin on her knees and held the doll against her legs, clasping her hands tightly around its midsection. "This is all I have left from my life in Savannah." Her mouth twisted sideways. "Not much, is it?"

He ran a gnarled finger down the doll's cheek and twisted

a fuzzy curl back into place. "You have all you need inside your heart. The memories will live, and home will always be with you."

She ran his words through her mind, just as she'd done every other time he'd imparted small pearls of wisdom. "Martin?" She listened to the rustling of his body as he lay down and pulled the blanket over him. She heard more rustling as he twisted and turned, trying to find a comfortable spot on the frozen earth.

"Hmmm?"

"Will I see Sally again?"

"Yes, Granddaughter. If you believe."

"Believe in what?"

"Yourself."

Sophia sat in her tucked position for so long her legs tingled painfully, but after a short while, the tingling stopped and her legs went numb. Sleep was as elusive as a possible change in the cold weather. Too many doubts and fears rattled around in her head. How could she go on? She'd never had to fend for herself before, which was a daunting thought. And if Major Todd was indeed haunting her…

Martin placed his hand against her leg and gave her a tiny squeeze. "I can hear your thoughts, Sophia. Do not worry so much. We will make a good family, I think."

"Will you really stay with me? I won't be alone?"

He squeezed her leg again, the only way he could comfort her in her guarded position. "No, Granddaughter. I will not leave you. My heart tells me our paths are meant to be together. Besides, who else will nag after me? Now curl up in your blanket and sleep. Morning will be here soon enough."

Sophia closed her eyes and listened to the night sounds around her. Somewhere on the other side of the camp's perimeter, a wolf barked out a quiet cough, but even that slowly faded away. She hovered on the ledge between sleep and wakefulness when a deep, taunting voice whispered in her ear.

"Dearest Sophia..."

Her eyes flew open and she bolted upright, trying to see where he was through the blanket of darkness surrounding her. Had she been dreaming? Holding her breath, she waited, but the only sound greeting her was a heavy cloak of silence. She forced herself to lie back down and huddled underneath the thin blanket as she tried to escape both the freezing air and her own apprehension. The rapid beating of her heart echoed inside her head. She felt a nearby presence and held her breath, willing away the terrifying sensation—when a gloved hand suddenly covered her nose and mouth.

"You think the old Indian can save you?" the major whispered. "He can't. Your future is with me, dearest Sophia."

She tried to shake her head, to tell him how wrong he was. She reached up with numb fingers and pulled at the hand clamped to her face. The more she tugged, however, the harder he pressed until a sharp sting seared through her lips as the dry skin split apart. She couldn't stop the tiny whimper of pain. She felt him lean closer...the evil within him was a physical entity hovering above her.

"Do you truly wish to lose your new Indian friends, too?" His hand pushed one last time, the back of her head grinding against the hard ground beneath her. Then just as abruptly as he'd appeared, he was gone. The sound of his demented laughter disappeared into the echoes of his horse's hooves clopping along the frozen ground.

She forced her fingers to relax from their severe grip on the blanket. She shivered uncontrollably, unsure if it was from fear or the surrounding cold.

CHAPTER 5

Near Vienna, Illinois

Sophia readjusted the pathetic blanket around her shoulders. In the week and a half since leaving Kentucky, she'd pushed Major Todd to the back of her mind. They'd seen less of Bryan, as well. He'd only been able to stop once to give them food. He had also verified that the major had indeed been placed in charge. Hearing that gave her a tiny bit of hope; he wouldn't have as much time to mess with her sanity because he'd had too many other things to deal with—like not getting everyone lost.

The clinking of harnesses and the frozen huffing of horses pulled her thoughts to the present. She turned to see two wounded-looking soldiers walking toward her, their faces swollen and covered with large purple welts. One soldier's arm was wrapped, and the other, his knee. Both bandages showed red blood seeping through the dirty gray cloths. They looked as though they'd been involved in a brawl.

She hadn't noticed the man draped across the back of one

of the horses until the men dumped him on the ground at her feet. A pain-filled moan drew her gaze downward. One glance at the unconscious man's face and she gasped. His eyes were swollen shut and sealed with blood. His nose was bent at an odd angle, and even more blood trailed from one nostril down the side of his face. His bloody lips had been split open several times, and she could see dark red welts crisscrossing his upper chest through the vee of his torn shirt.

She jerked her gaze from the pitiful man and glared at the soldiers who had already remounted their horses. She thrust her small fists onto each hip and glared. "What have you done to him? He's almost dead!" she yelled at the retreating figures.

Martin shuffled up behind her and glanced down. A drawn-out, strangled sound came from him, and he fell beside the man. His aged fingers tenderly brushed the stranger's matted black hair from his forehead.

She knelt by Martin's side. "Do you know this man?"

His voice was so quiet, she had to lean forward to hear him. His worry beat at her. "Yes. This is Clay."

"The man who came to see you at the stockade? This is *that* Clay?" When Martin nodded, she groaned then stood. Tugging on the older man's arm, she helped him to his feet. "Come on. I'll need help lifting him into the wagon so I can tend his wounds, but I can't promise it will help. Some of them look as if they're festering."

With help from several Indian boys, the younger children were removed from the wagon and Clay now lay in their place. Sophia felt sorry for the little ones now having to walk, but the man was simply too injured and there wasn't enough room for everyone.

As Martin sat with Clay, she pulled out their small bucket, holding what little water they had left from the last stream they'd crossed. The bucket was a priceless gift from Bryan that he'd brought them after he'd realized they were unable to store water. Thankfully, snow was only frozen water. She ran to a nearby tree and pulled down a branch, catching as much of the falling snow in the bucket as she could. She placed it beside Clay then pulled the ruffle off the bottom of her skirt and ripped it into several long strips. She tried to clean as much of the blood from Clay's face as she could, then started on his chest while Martin reset Clay's broken nose.

She gazed at the man's poor face. He looked terrible. Rousing herself, she dipped one of the cleaner strips of material into the melted snow and gently wiped the lacerated bits of flesh that had once been lips. She continued the routine, afraid to stop but unsure what to do next. She had never taken care of someone this injured.

Slowly, Clay became aware of someone touching him, rubbing something ice-cold over his sensitive mouth, the movement so soft. His body felt heavy and sore, and the simple act of swallowing sapped any stored energy. The wet cloth touched the inflamed skin on his chest, each movement feathering over him like a calming breeze.

He tried to talk, wanting to ask who it was helping him, but gentle fingers lightly touched his lips, and a soft, sultry voice whispered near his ear.

"You are safe now. Sleep." The quiet admonition was the last thing he heard, and for the first time since he'd been attacked, he fell into a normal, restful asleep.

Sophia jerked awake from her wonderful dream. Gone were the elegant gowns and beautiful people, and in their place—

whispers. Raspy, horrible sounds she knew were meant to terrify her. It worked. This time, however, something was different. The whispers came closer. She heard the familiar scraping of boots against the rocky earth on the other side of the wagon bed where she lay.

"*Sophia...*" A tiny whimper escaped from her paralyzed body. *"You're no longer alone, dearest Sophia. Soon, I will have you all to myself."* The singsong voice faded, and she let out her restrained sigh, only to choke on it again when a hand appeared from the dark shadows, hovering above the wagon's protective wall.

Before the gloved apparition could grab her, her terrified squeal woke Martin, who jerked into a sitting position. "Who's there? Show yourself!" The last either one of them heard was a pair of boots scuffling away from them.

"When were you going to tell me? How long has he been tormenting you?" he asked.

She winced at the angry tone lacing each word and crawled to the end of the wagon bed, letting her legs dangle over the edge. With his accusatory glares, she knew she was in for a lecture. "I'm sorry, Martin. I thought I could handle the major on my own, but now I know I should have told you first. There's something wrong with his mind."

Martin gave a loud *grunt,* then scooted closer to her on the end of the wagon. "Sophia, I thought you understood how sick the man was after what he did to you back at the fort. I have tried to watch out for you, and young Bryan is also helping. He watches both of you, but he can't be everywhere." He leaned closer and took her chilled hand in his, gently rubbing the back side with his calloused thumb. "You *must* tell us when something happens—no matter how minor you think it may be. Do you understand the importance of what I'm telling you?"

Taking care of Clay had kept her mind off her worries,

but the terrifying incident brought them all rushing back. She stole a quick glance at the sleeping form; his only movement was the occasional jerk of his muscles. She met Martin's concerned gaze. With his dark gray brows bunched together, his wrinkles seemed more prominent. "I understand," she whispered, the constant shivers shaking her too-thin shoulders.

Shifting in the wagon's tight space, she turned toward Clay, not wanting to meet Martin's troubled stare. She sighed in frustration. Would their problems never end? She wasn't as naïve as Martin and Bryan seemed to think she was. She knew quite well what evils Major Todd was capable of. But she would keep her promise to Martin and let him or Bryan know the next time the major tried something.

She stared at the discolorations on Clay's face. His eyes moved back and forth behind his closed lids and his dark brown eyebrows bunched, the ridges in the skin between them forming prominent furrows. His body jerked several times. She laid her hand over his heart and was surprised when he immediately calmed, resuming a more peaceful slumber. Leaning closer, she placed the back of her hand against Clay's forehead to make sure his fever hadn't returned.

Frustrated she couldn't do more for him, she re-tucked the threadbare army blanket around Clay's shoulders and beneath his chin. There weren't enough blankets for everybody, and the limited amount available were no better than the rags the house staff used for cleaning back home. So many Cherokee had died, which she now believed had been the government's plan all along.

Her empty stomach rumbled in protest. Her last meal had been the previous morning. Just like the blanket supply, their meager rations couldn't feed everyone. They'd come up with a plan for alternating meals so that every person ate at least once a day, but she didn't always adhere to that plan...especially when she caught sight of the children who suffered even more than she. At least she understood why there was so little food. Most of them were too young to comprehend.

A movement beside the wagon caught her attention, and she watched two young children walking together, guarded on either side by their parents as they passed. A small smile touched her face when she realized their tiny frames didn't look quite as skeletal as they had several weeks before. If going hungry meant saving more children, she would gladly give up some of her food.

Taking one last glance at Clay, she turned and crawled back to the end of the wagon, climbing out to join Martin. Several feet away, he'd built a small fire for cooking their meager breakfast of mealy flour biscuits and salt pork. Staring into the dancing orange flames, she winced when she rubbed her hands together. She'd been cold for so long, even a tiny bit of heat burned.

"I am so very tired of feeling frozen. I want my bed back home so I can burrow under the warm coverlet," she complained. "I can't even begin to remember what it felt like, the constant heat from the fireplace in my bedroom. I miss home." As her eyes closed from exhaustion, something hard pressed into her cupped palms. She glanced down and saw a small hardtack biscuit lying there. She frowned and raised her head to meet Martin's worried gaze.

"You are getting too thin, Granddaughter. You spend all your time taking care of Clay and me, and you forget yourself. There was an extra biscuit this morning. Everyone agreed you should have it." He held up his gnarled hand before she could turn him down. "Do not think I haven't seen how many times you have given your meal to the young ones. Honor Jesse's passing last night and eat the biscuit."

So many friends had died on this godforsaken trip.

Sophia felt the heavy pain of grief as tears filled her eyes once again. A quiet greeting broke their tense silence, and she glanced up to see Bryan step up to their small fire, looking tired and dirty. Sophia curled her nose, knowing she must look the same. She would have given just about anything for a quick dip in a stream, although she'd probably freeze before she could get out.

She and Martin patiently waited while the young soldier squatted and took off his hat, then with a well-practiced motion, ran his fingers through his rather shaggy reddish-brown hair. He thrust a small wrapped bundle into her hands. "Here, Miss Sophia. I saved these for you an' Mr. Jefferson. I 'magine he's right tired of the broth you've been feedin' him. If he ever wakes up, he's gonna be hungry." Mindful of his gaze as she carefully unwrapped the parcel, her expression turned from curiosity to suspicion to concern as her eyebrows drew together in a frown. As if knowing where her thoughts had turned, he held up a hand. "Don't worry on my account. I watched those two new soldiers. When they didn't eat everything, I took what was left. I'd a been here sooner, but the major's carryin' on something fierce—all possessed like, if'n you know what I mean."

Sophia made a very unladylike grunting sound. "I know exactly what you mean." She paused and took a long breath. She understood the risks Bryan took on their behalf—stealing the food—and knew if he were caught, the punishment would be severe. "How will we ever repay you for all you've done?" Even in the dim light, she could see the red blush spreading across his face.

"Aw, shucks, Miss Sophia. My mamma would have my backside if I didn't help you. It's not right, what's happenin' to the Indians. Besides, you'd do the same for me." Bryan jumped up and jammed his hat back down onto his head, making the hair around his ears stick out more than usual. "I need to get back before they notice I'm gone." He took a few hurried steps away from their small camp...then returned, his face scrunched into a thoughtful frown. "I'm not rightly sure what the major's carryin' on about, but my gut tells me you need to be careful, Miss Sophia. Stick close to Martin, an' keep your eyes open." His blue eyes hardened, reminding her of the flash of a gem in bright sunlight. "Don't you take *any* chances, you hear?"

With a quick nod, she stood and laid her hand over his dirty coat sleeve. Leaning forward, she placed a quick kiss on his cheek. His short stubble tickled her lips. Biting back a smile when his face flamed red again, she whispered, "Be safe yourself—and thank you."

He mumbled something unintelligible under his breath as he ducked his head and hurried away.

Propped up on one elbow, Clay watched the beautiful woman lean forward and kiss the soldier on the cheek. He recognized the girl from the few times he'd awakened to find her caring for him. With her attention on the soldier, he took a few moments to study her. She was truly beautiful. Her long dark brown hair was pulled back in a messy braid that hung down the middle of her back. Like the Indians surrounding them, she was too thin. An army blanket was wrapped around her shoulders. He could see the stains on her long skirt, which he knew from experience hadn't been washed since she was rounded up like everyone else. The hem of her skirt was unusually short...he glanced down at the makeshift sling binding his arm and realized she'd used the ruffle on him.

Staring at her, his gaze traced the elegant curve of her neck and her straight nose. She had full lips and wide eyes...

dark brown if he remembered correctly. She was beautiful, reminding him a little of Martin's daughter.

His uninjured shoulder trembled from the strain of holding up the weight of his upper body, and he slowly eased himself back down. He pulled the blanket up with his good hand and stared up at the purplish-pink streaks crossing the sky as the new day dawned. Sparse patches of midnight blue faded, oblivious to the still-glowing white stars blinking their unknown song—but he didn't see them as his thoughts turned back to the woman, wondering again who she was.

He knew he should be thinking about how to escape so he could return to the search for the men who killed his family. He needed to find justice for their deaths before he could return to his job as a Lighthorseman—his people's version of the legal system. He'd left the other five men in his patrol to take care of their assigned district, but by now they would be worried. He should have already returned home.

A soft peal of laughter floated toward him, and the puckered skin between his brows ached as his scowl deepened. His current situation was maddening, and what he should be thinking about was finding his horse and returning to his search…yet all he wanted to think about was the woman's beautiful face and kind nature.

Now that he'd fulfilled his duty to Martin as his father's best friend, nothing had been gained. His efforts hadn't changed the outcome for the Cherokee people. The plan had been ideal—go to the forts and stockades where the Indians were being held and gather information regarding their welfare…and at the same time, spy on the soldiers manning the forts. He'd hoped to find information regarding his family's murderers, but he'd failed to find even a hint of their names. It had been a long shot, but he'd tried.

He stared at the end of the wagon and found himself waiting for the beautiful woman to appear. Several minutes ticked by until he realized what he was doing. Closing his eyes, he shook his head and inhaled, slowly pushing the air from his lungs as he willed his sore muscles to relax and his mind to go blank.

Just before he allowed himself to slip into a light sleep, he heard her scramble into the back of the wagon. His lips twitched as she mumbled and grunted, trying to find a comfortable position next to him. When he heard a *thud* and then a very unladylike response, a hoarse chuckle, which sounded more like the croaking of a frog, broke through his pinched lips.

"Oh! You're awake."

His eyelids popped open when he felt the cool breeze of her movement as she moved away. He felt the soft touch of something against his abdomen. Even with her feather-light push, it still felt as if she'd shoved the butt of a gun into his midsection, and he could do nothing to stop his groan of pain.

She gasped and her gaze flew to his. Even dirt-smudged, she was breathtaking. Long, dark strands of brown hair had pulled free from the long braid draped over one shoulder, the end tied with a torn piece of muslin. She was so close, he could see the small black specks inside the rich brown pools of her eyes, which were opened wide.

He grabbed the tiny wrist, stopping her circular motions. She jerked back as if struck, and dropped whatever she'd been holding in her other hand. His eyes narrowed as she tried to pull her arm away. He winced as the jolting movement sent a fresh wave of pain through him.

"I'm sorry if I pressed too hard, or hurt you," she whispered. He let go of her wrist, noticing the way she scooted away from him.

"It's not your fault. I startled you," he said through clenched teeth, his voice strained. He let his arm slide down to the rough wagon planks underneath him and felt around for the two small objects she'd dropped. His long fingers found them, and after two tries, he managed to pick them up. He held them out to her. "I think you dropped these."

"Yes. Your meal, I'm afraid." He heard her small sigh but stayed silent. "The soldiers keep most of the food for themselves, so a group of us share what we do get. A young soldier, Bryan MacConnell, has helped by giving us extra water and stealing food whenever he can. I brought you two hardtack biscuits."

He raised them to his nose and sniffed, wincing at the bitter odor. "Do they taste as bad as they smell?"

She laughed. "Worse. But you'll get used to them, especially the hungrier you get. Eat those two, and if you're still hungry, I have a few more. You can thank Bryan for your feast. He knew you'd be hungry as soon as you woke up."

He took a bite of the hard bread and chewed quickly, trying to breathe as much as he could through his still-swollen nose. They really did taste as bad as they smelled. He was surprised when she turned away and lay down beside him.

"Get some sleep. Martin and I have been taking turns watching over you, which means the one not in here is out there. Walking. For hours."

Clay stared at the back of her head. The healing cut on his lip split open again as he smiled.

THE MOMENT SOPHIA woke and saw Martin's flushed face, she knew something was wrong. During the day, he never willingly climbed into the wagon. She leaned over Clay, trying not to touch his sleeping body. She forced her hand away and pressed it against Martin's cheek. He was burning up. A tight squeezing seized her insides.

Martin tried to smile and pulled her hand down, but kept a loose hold on her cool fingers. "Do not worry so. If the Great Spirit wants me, I will have no choice but to go."

When she replied, her voice sounded squeaky and unused. "Grandfather, you can't leave me too. You promised me we would stay together...as a family. I refuse to let you slip away so easily. Promise me you will fight to get better?" Her fear spiked a little more when she heard the rattling intake of air as he drew in a breath. "Please?" she whispered.

A smile broke through the many wrinkles covering his face. "I'm not going anywhere at the moment." He patted her small hand with his larger one. "Do not worry so."

The frantic rhythm of her heart calmed. "You already said that." Her lips twitched but she couldn't stop the hard shiver that shook her thin frame. Tiny chips of ice hidden in the strong winter wind hit her face, and the cold seeped into her bones. "But I will try." Talking was difficult as her teeth clicked together in the midday's chill.

He gave her a halfhearted wave. "I will be fine. While the wagons are not moving, go and take care of your needs." As she hopped to the ground, his weak voice carried a warning. "Do not go far into the woods, and do not go alone."

Sophia glanced back into the wagon, searching Clay's sleeping face. He looked rested, actually peaceful—until his eyes opened and he grimaced.

"I don't think I've ever felt this cold before," he muttered "I think there's a hive of bees stinging my feet and hands."

She chuckled then leaned against the wagon bed's rough wooden slats. "I know that pain well. Not only do I feel it now, but when I was five, my best friend took me creek jumping."

His laugh was deep, its rich baritone bubbling through her. "And you fell in," he added.

"Unfortunately, yes. We were young and full of adventure.

We also didn't know what to look out for when choosing a jumping-in spot. If we had, the large hive hanging from a large tree limb high above our heads would've been the first thing we saw. Instead, it blended in perfectly with the surrounding leaves, and I found out the hard way that bees don't like a lot of noise…or heat…or water. It makes them cranky." She paused, remembering that day with a mixture of fondness and regret. "I don't recall ever feeling pain like that. Mamma Lou—my nanny—counted more than twenty-seven stings. Thomas had even more."

When Clay met her gaze, she felt as if she were falling into a deep pit. Unlike anyone else in her life, for whatever reason, this man touched something inside her—and it scared her.

"Who is Thomas?" The richness of his voice sent a wave of tingly prickles over her skin, making her want to hear him talk again.

"He's Mamma Lou's oldest child and was one of my best friends."

His brow rose. "Was? He's dead?"

She shrugged. "I don't know. He was sold to another plantation. My mother didn't like that I had befriended a Negro boy. She said he was beneath me and that I was never to talk to him again." That particular memory had always bothered her. She had, of course, spent time with him after that…until one morning when he was simply gone. Not even Mamma Lou would talk about her son. She squirmed, needing to relieve herself but didn't want to stop what she was doing. Talking with Clay was nice, and she didn't want the feeling to end. "Martin said you are a kind of lawman for your tribe?"

He nodded. "A Lighthorseman. There are three tribal districts in the Choctaw culture with six Lighthorsemen assigned to each district. I am the captain of my group."

"I understood from Martin you're like a sheriff, but what exactly do you do?"

"If you compare us to the white form of law, I guess we are the judge, jury, and executioner all rolled into one."

"And what if you make a mistake? Hunt down an innocent person?" she asked, a slight frown tugging at her shapely brows.

"We make certain we have the right person, but we are human. Unfortunately, mistakes are made."

She stood, her bladder's discomfort turning to a sharp pain. "I need to go…take care of a few things. Do you need anything before I leave?"

He shook his head and closed his eyes. "No, but thank you for asking."

Fearing her bladder would burst, she didn't waste any more time and hurried toward the tree line, unsure as to why her insides tingled when she was with Clay. She enjoyed Bryan's company immensely, but when she was with Clay… She turned her attention the task at hand and quickly relieved herself. Straightening her skirt, she wished nature provided a better privy.

Stepping away from behind the tree she'd used, Sophia looked around for her first landmark leading back to camp. She avoided stepping on the many sticks littering the ground, preferring the softer ground underneath her worn moccasins. She was surprised at how easy it had been for her to adjust to the more simple ways of the Cherokee, which had quickly become like second nature to her.

Just as she found the final marker, a loud *crack* sounded behind her. She jerked to a stop, her heartbeat accelerating uncomfortably as it pounded against her ribs. Another twig snapped, the sound nearer, and she threw herself backward against the closest tree. Luckily, it was one of the larger ones and afforded her enough cover.

Stupid, stupid, stupid. Why didn't I listen to Martin? She forced air through her nose as quietly as she could, every noise around her sounding ominous. It would've taken her only five seconds to grab one of the women to go with her—but all she could do now was kick herself for her stupidity. Her muscles tensed when another branch cracked right behind the tree where she hid.

Trying to calm the frantic pounding of her heart was impossible. The eerie silence of the woods pressed in around her, her nerves quickly fraying. Pressed against the rough bark of the tree for what seemed like hours instead of only a few minutes, she tried to convince herself that whoever it had been was now gone...until a familiar tune whistled through the air. The singsong cadence pushed at a distant memory, but she couldn't remember where she'd heard it before. Her tensed muscles ached, and an incessant quivering increased in her arms and legs the longer she held her stiff position.

As quick as a wink, she remembered where she'd heard the tune. It was one of her father's favorite sea shanties that he used to sing to her when she was little. There was only one person in this godforsaken wilderness who had known her father. She thought she'd understood fear and how it felt, but this new surge of emotion went beyond that. Truly petrified and with no idea what to do, she whispered a prayer under her breath.

The decision about what she should do was ripped from her when a hand dropped onto her shoulder. Emitting a loud squeal, she bolted forward and didn't stop. Her pent-up terror propelled her through the trees and into Bryan's arms at the edge of the clearing, where he'd evidently been waiting for her.

"What...?" His grip tightened around her as she violently shook in his arms. He just held her until she finally stopped trembling. She gently pushed against his chest. He let her step away from him, but continued to hold her at arm's length. One look at her face and he muttered a curse under his breath. "What happened?" he growled.

Sophia closed her eyes and drew in as much air as her lungs would hold, then slowly released it, along with the majority of her fear. For now, at least, she was safe. A relieved smile slowly spread, but when she opened her eyes, her relief changed to chagrin at the sight of Bryan's angry glower. "It seems like all I do is apologize to everyone, but I'm sorry. I was concerned about something else and completely forgot Martin's warning."

She fell into step beside him as he turned and walked her back to the wagon. Some of her fear returned when she thought about the major. "Bryan, he tried to grab me." She shook her head. "What am I going to do?"

He helped her into the wagon, where she promptly covered Martin's bronzed cheek with the back of her hand. He was still burning up. She wished she knew how to make him better.

Clay's voice whispered behind her, husky from sleep. "You need rest too, Sophia. Bryan has a job to do."

The young soldier cleared his throat. "Um, I was comin' to tell you 'bout the regular driver. The major thought one of 'em looked a little dark and dismissed the lot. I'm your driver now."

Clay grunted. "Well, there you go. Bryan can drive the wagon. Now go to sleep, Sophia."

The sound of her name pouring off his tongue was musical, and her heart did a funny little dance inside her chest. At least during the day there would be no strange whispers, and she would be able to sleep a lot better.

CHAPTER 6

"This is a nice way to wake up."

Sophia's eyes popped open as she stared into Clay's shadowy dark-chocolate ones. Mesmerized, she let her gaze follow his lips as they rose into a knowing grin. She scrambled into a sitting position, but promptly lost her balance and fell back onto the object of her discomfort. Clay.

Could this get any worse? Horrified, and with jumbled nerves, she couldn't get her brain to think straight. She tried to ignore Clay's low chuckle as she tried for a second time to push herself off his chest...his wonderfully hard, muscled chest.

"Oh, just stop it," she muttered to herself.

"I haven't done anything."

Her gaze flew up to meet his, and he grinned wider. "Ohhh!" She gave him her best glare and scooted to the end of the wagon.

"It's a woman thing, Clay." Martin chuckled from the other side of their small, shared space. "My Klara did the same thing. She talked to herself whenever she got agitated or embarrassed."

"You are not helping, Martin," she said without looking back. She jerked her skirt from where it was wrapped around her foot and pushed herself out of the motionless wagon. She needed to put some distance between herself and Mr. Clay Jefferson.

After helping to gather the children, she decided to walk the trail for a while, letting a few of the children take her place inside the wagon. She had just set the last child between Clay's feet when a movement beside him caught her attention. She looked over and saw Martin trying to crawl toward the end of the wagon. With one hand on each hip, she stood in his way. "Oh no, you don't."

"I do not need to be lying here while the children walk," he said, his voice sounding tired and drained. "According to Bryan, the large river ahead is icy and dangerous. I could never forgive myself if something were to happen."

Sophia kissed his hot cheek, her palms quickly warming against his chest. "You are not going anywhere, Grandfather. Your fever has gotten worse. To get better, you need lots of rest." She gently pushed him back to his original spot. "So rest."

"But..."

She shook her head, resting one hand on his lower leg. "No. You will remain here." Her grip tightened. "I cannot lose you too," she whispered. For a moment, Martin didn't move. Then without a word, he leaned against the wall behind him and crossed his legs with a nod.

She smiled gratefully and held onto the other side of the wagon as Bryan clicked to the horses, beginning another day's journey.

THE MISSISSIPPI RIVER. She couldn't seem to blink, and knew she probably looked like an owl as she stared at the ice-congested water. The longer her gaze continued to sweep the watery horizon, the faster her heart stuttered as the ball of fear inside her chest grew. "We can't cross that," she whispered. A frigid blast of wind from the river hit her raw skin. "That's not a river…it's an ocean." They had already crossed two decent-sized rivers since beginning this trek, but this…

Clay's deep voice startled her, and she was finally able to pull her gaze away and onto his lean face as he stepped up beside her. "They call this the Mighty Mississippi, and you're right. These waters are hard to cross in good weather. Frozen? It's deadly."

She frowned up at him. "You shouldn't be up, Clay. Your body hasn't fully healed. Tiring yourself won't help."

His lips drew together in a straight line. From the corner of her eye, she noticed the clenching and unclenching of his jaws. His scowl sharpened his features even more, but to her, he reminded her of a fierce warrior ready for battle. She bit back a chuckle. *Well, at least what I think a warrior should look like.* Reluctantly, she turned her gaze back to the turbulent river. "How will we cross?"

Clay pulled his blanket tighter, his shoulder bumping into hers, when a strong wind blew into them. "Last night, Bryan told us a soldier had been dispatched with orders to commandeer no less than three large paddleboats. With luck, they should be here sometime today. If not, we'll be camping here until they do."

He turned to face her and let out a frustrated sigh as her shivering body convulsed against his. "If you shake any harder, you're going to break something." He wrapped his hand around her upper arm and winced.

"What?"

He frowned down at her. "It's as if I'm holding a small stick and not your arm. While we're stopped, crawl up into the wagon and get warm."

She threw him a questioning glance, and he chuckled. "Well, at least you will be out of this wind."

She stood her ground, which was difficult to do against the freezing barrage of air gusts. "I'm not getting into the wagon unless you do too. You've been ill. I haven't."

"Yet," he bit out. "I've watched you take care of everyone else, including me, leaving no time for yourself." His tone deepened with a husky rasp the longer he talked. "You are like the coyote, adaptable and protective, yet your own feelings remain a secret." His hair brushed the tops of his shoulders as he shook his head. "If I didn't know better, I'd think you were an Indian maid."

She didn't know if he was joking or not. "Why?" His face changed completely when his lips rose into a full smile. She sucked in a quick breath at the transformation. He was so handsome.

"You're bossy." His chuckle sent tingles down her neck and arms. Where his hand gripped her, the tingles disappeared into the escalating temperature of her skin.

To keep her safe from herself and what she wanted to do —which was to kiss him—Sophia pulled her arm from his grasp and scrambled up into the wagon bed. The only spot left open in the crowded wagon was where Clay had slept. She had curled up and closed her eyes, willing her heart to slow down, when something bumped her leg. A very large something.

Her eyes flew open, and her gaze landed on Clay, who had squeezed in beside her and curled up in a very awkward and clearly uncomfortable position. Staring at him didn't help her frantically thumping heart, so after a quick inhalation of frigid air, she laid her hand on his partially blanketed shoulder.

Clay's head jerked sideways, his brown eyes wide and surprised. "What's wrong?"

"You can't sleep like that."

One dark brow rose. "What would you suggest, my dear?"

His voice had her nerves dancing merrily, but when she heard the oddly familiar endearment, a flame of anger burst through her head, making her feel lightheaded and dizzy. All humor drained away, and she pinned his gaze to hers. "Don't *ever* call me dear in any fashion. Do you understand?"

He held still, his expression and gaze void of emotion. "Why?"

She took several calming breaths before trying to explain, feeling a bit foolish for her outburst. "Let's just say another person has used it too much for my comfort." From the hard glint flashing through his eyes, she knew he understood.

"Sophia."

The sound of her name flowing off his tongue melted away her anger. A soft, fluttery sensation spread through her chest. The man could shatter her world if she let him. Her eyelids closed as she pretended to stifle a yawn and changed the subject. "You can't sleep in that position because you're still healing. Lying curled up and twisted will make your condition worse."

"Why?"

She met his amused stare. *Insolent man*. The fluttering in her chest quickened. Raising her brows high on her forehead, she pushed out her chin and gave him her best haughty expression, which she got from her mother. "I don't know," she bit out. "Stop asking questions and go to sleep."

His stomach-plunging smile never faltered as he slowly scooted toward her. "Move down." She did what he said and scooted a few inches toward the end of the wagon. "Closer." His eyes dared her to obey.

Weighing her choices, she quickly realized she had none. She maneuvered her cold limbs toward his prone form.

TRAIL OF HOPE

When his hand suddenly snaked around her waist and pulled her the final few inches, she jumped but found herself wrapped in his warm embrace. He was right, she admitted silently. This was better than standing out in the arctic wind and freezing.

The sounds of ice breaking in the river and the occasional child's snuffle proved a powerful sleeping draught, even allowing her to forget about the hard body pressed against her. Clay's deep, rhythmic breathing made her feel safe and lulled her into a light sleep. As her mind shut down, several thoughts slipped through the murky haze. She liked the feeling of freedom, as if her world had righted itself again.

For the first time since her capture, the too-tight pull of her neck and shoulder muscles from constant worry faded. She wanted to let herself enjoy the moment, but the practical side of her mind wasn't going to let her. The last thing she needed was for him to find out just how much she already cared for him. A quiet whisper tickled her ear as the outside world faded.

"Thank you, *aiukli*." The strange word flowed like a short melody.

She stared up into the cloud-covered sky and listened to the soft puffs of air coming from the sleeping man beside her and dared to hope. Was it possible he might care for her too?

Sophia's eyes cracked open to the graying light of early evening. She was so ready for spring. Listening to the familiar sounds of life on the other side of their wagon wall gave her the chance to think. So many things had happened to her. That fateful night seemed like a lifetime ago. With a start, she realized that was exactly what it was. It was as if her past were no longer her own, and had become someone else's life. With no home or real family to call her own, her future looked bleak.

Clay moved behind her, pushing his body against her back. Her breath caught in her throat. Her stomach did a funny flip-flop as a burning excitement flooded her warm body. With some difficulty, she tamped down the unfamiliar sensations. She couldn't help but realize how comfortable she was with him. The only other males to have her hard-earned trust had been her father, Martin, and Bryan. *Did she trust Clay?*

Warmth encased her heart as she thought about Martin and how wonderful the elderly man was to her and everyone else. From the beginning, he'd been good to her. She truly wished she could be his granddaughter. Her thoughts turned once again to Clay. Did he ever think about her? His teasing seemed more brotherly than anything else. She sighed, irritated with herself as her mind realized what her heart already had. She may have only known Clay Jefferson a short while, but she was in love with him.

"That sigh sounded sad. Is something wrong?"

Well, shoot, she thought. *Now what am I going to say?* She suppressed a hard shiver when a frigid burst of wind shot through the rickety wooden walls of the wagon. "Nothing's wrong. Just relaxing." The words tumbled over each other, and she hoped he would accept her answer and not press the issue. She breathed in a slow, silent sigh of relief when his mind turned to something else.

"Has…Martin said anything to you about crossing the river?"

She wondered at the slight hesitation in his voice. "No, he hasn't. Well, other than we need to pay close attention to the ice and the children. He's worried one of them will fall in." Unthinking, she rolled onto her back and found herself looking up into his dark eyes. Bottomless pools of ink. Mentally kicking herself, she forced the next question between her frozen lips. "Why does the ice worry everyone?"

His eyes lowered to her mouth, and she forgot to breathe. When he answered, her lungs remembered to do their job, and she gulped in air.

"With the weather warming up, even by only a couple of degrees, the ice breaks apart. As the ship pushes through the water, the larger chunks ram the sides, making it very dangerous. If a large or sharp enough piece hits, the ship's wooden hull will have a nice new hole in it."

She bunched her eyebrows. "That wouldn't be good," she whispered.

An amused smirk covered his face. "No," he agreed with a chuckle. "That would not be good. You worry too much. We'll cross safely." He leaned over and brushed his lips over hers, then he sat up and scooted out of the wagon, seemingly unaware of what he'd just done.

She lay still, her gaze staring into the heavy, gray clouds blanketing the overhead sky. Torrents of rain or heavy snow could have dropped on her, and she wouldn't have cared. He'd kissed her. She ran the tips of her quickly cooling fingers across her lips, where the memory of his soft kiss lingered. Deep voices slipped into her bemused mind and rapidly drew her attention as their conversation became clear.

"...the townspeople complained, and we were moved here. Martin, *here* isn't a good place to be. Moccasin Springs is hard enough to cross in calm weather, but now? Look around you. The Cherokee are in no shape to battle anything. Those who aren't sick soon will be. The trip to the new territory is barely half over, and thousands are dead already." Even though she was unable to see his face, Sophia could hear the depth of Clay's concern resonating in each word.

After a long pause, Martin's equally deep, gravelly voice responded. "What is it you are not saying, Nighthawk? We have no choice but to do what the soldiers tell us."

Nighthawk. She'd forgotten about his Choctaw name, rightfully fitting his darker, more restless spirit. She'd often wondered why he seemed so driven. The stiff way he held himself and his frequent jaw clenching made her wonder what terrible memories were going through his mind. His eyes looked haunted. Maybe one day he'd trust her enough to tell her what chewed at his insides.

"Bryan told me about Todd being placed in command when Jackson was called back to Washington. Why didn't you tell me? The man's an idiot. He'll get us all killed before we get near the Territory!"

When she heard Todd's name, a strangled mewling escaped her frozen lips. She whipped a hand over her mouth and held her breath, only letting it out when Clay resumed his low-pitched conversation.

"When the Choctaw crossed this river, it was summer. We had calm weather with only a light breeze pushing the boats. Even then, one of the boats drifted off course. For days, we camped by the river's edge, but the boat never returned. Our leader's incompetence cost my family their lives! If the boat had arrived when it should have, my mother, father, and… and," Clay's voice broke and he cleared his throat. "My sister would never have been murdered."

She was so enthralled with Clay's story and the loss of so many people, she never felt the twin streams of salty tears running down her cheeks. She understood so much now, and could not fault his reticence. Wrapped up in her sad thoughts, she missed the first part of Martin's response.

"…not know why the Great Spirit calls home those we

love. We cannot question his wisdom, my son. I, too, lost that day. I loved your sister as my own granddaughter. Both my girls were taken too young. You know what I need from you. You do not have to say anything right now, but the one story I've longed to hear—needed to hear—has never been told to me."

Clay was silent for a moment then took a deep breath. "You want to know what happened to my father."

"Yes. He was my brother in spirit—my blood brother."

"Father used to tell tales about the two of you." A low chuckle sounded, but she couldn't tell whose it was. "He used to say you would be a perfect Indian if only you'd been Choctaw."

"I used to say the same about him, only the other way around. I've missed his jokes, his counsel."

"It happened several days after the ship disappeared. We were camped near the river to wait. Mother never gave up hope that her parents and friends would return. Ribbons of yellow and pink still decorated the morning sky when I left to get our daily rations at the army camp several miles ahead. It wasn't safe to send my mother or sister with so many soldiers around, so I went in their place. When I returned, I found them lying on the ground. My father's body shielded them, and the only thing I could see of my sister was her foot sticking out from underneath. She wore her new beaded moccasins. *Ishki*, Mother, had a devil of a time getting Susan to sit down. All my sister wanted to do was follow me around and learn to hunt. Just before they died, Susan managed to sew her first pair of moccasins—it was either that or go barefoot." He chuckled. "She managed to sew a pair that actually stayed together and the beads didn't fall off."

Martin cleared his throat. "My brother died a warrior. He died trying to save his family. It is what he would have wanted." Sophia heard the pain and loss in his voice, and her heart ached for everything the two men had lost.

"I vowed that day that I would find who killed them," Clay said. "I *will* get justice for my family."

"It is good you want to avenge their deaths, but I think there's more than just vengeance in your heart. Be careful, young Nighthawk, that those roots don't grow so deep you are unable to make room for other feelings."

She held her breath until her lungs burned, but their silence continued. She crawled to the end of the wagon bed and lightly hopped to the ground. Two steps and a sharp turn around the wagon, and she found herself standing beside Martin's still form. Whether he was asleep or not, she couldn't tell. Clay still sat on the ground, his legs crossed at the ankles, unmoving. He raised his head but didn't look at her; instead, he gazed up into the darkening heavens. She glanced up as the gray clouds were quickly consumed, turning into an ominous ridge of cresting and whirling winds as the storm clouds gained control of the morning sky.

"Martin is the only family I have left. Because of their blood vow, I now take care of him instead of my father."

The small distance between them didn't dampen the waves of sadness she felt radiating from him. Seeing his vulnerability made her uncomfortable, her own heartache and too fresh. She clenched her fists together, her feet refusing to move forward to offer him comfort.

"Martin and my father were best friends, inseparable until Martin went to school." He lowered his head and looked over at the sleeping man.

Giving in to her heart, she leaned forward and placed a hand on his arm. "I'm so sorry, Clay. I can't imagine what you have been through."

"Mmm." She watched as he raised his other arm, his long fingers rubbing his eyes as the first large drops of rain began to fall. "At least my parents died with the hope that their son was still alive."

SEVERAL DAYS LATER, three ships arrived to carry them across the Mississippi. Getting everything loaded and ready to sail had been a trial, but the experience was worth it. Excitement coursed through Sophia as she looked out across the ice-laden swells. Unfortunately, the air was even colder on the water...land couldn't come soon enough. Her mind wandered back to Clay and what he would do once the army left. Engrossed in her thoughts, she didn't hear him join her at the ship's railing.

"What are you thinking about?"

The sound of his deep voice beside her made her jump. Fist clutched to her heart, she glared at him. "You scared me half to death." Ignoring his rich chuckle, she gripped the railing with her hands until her knuckles turned white. "I wasn't thinking about anything in particular."

Two large chunks of floating ice banged against each other while she hesitated. "My parents were killed too. My mother's death was suspicious—a broken neck in an empty room." She sighed. "My father? I'm not certain, but in my heart I know he's dead, too." Her eyes filled with unshed tears. "I miss him every day."

Clay looked at her with a furrowed brow. "What about your mother?"

Shrugging, she shook her head. "My mother was—different. She was the queen of tantrums. Whatever she wanted, she got." Her sharp laugh was bitter. "We were not close."

Clay remained silent. The boat's rocking motion sharpened, and her stomach moved along with it. Not only was the rebellious organ swaying from side to side but up and down and back and forth. With each passing second, that dance grew wilder.

Before she embarrassed herself, she braced herself with straightened arms on the railing and studied the different-sized chunks of ice. Taking slow, deep breaths, she concentrated on the river's wild beauty while her stomach regained its balance. The ice chunks mesmerized her, and she studied a sharp staircase pattern in the water. Her gaze traveled further out over the large expanse when two dark objects bobbed on the water's surface. At first she thought it was a large bird, but as the ship inched forward, the object turned, and she saw a weathered face. Her horror grew when she realized she was seeing people in the icy water. Sophia's heart fell when the second object turned, and she could see the child's beautiful but terrified face as it came into view.

"Oh no!" she gasped, grabbing for his arm. "Clay, there are people in the water!" Using the motion of the ship, her adrenalin propelled her forward. With no thoughts to her own safety, she threw herself over the ship's side and dropped into the freezing water.

The water crashed over her like an arctic blast, stinging her skin and sucking the small reserve of oxygen from her lungs. Struggling for air, she thrashed her way up through the river's strong pull from the ship's forward movement. With one last, hard kick, she broke through to the surface and drew in as much air as she could while her legs pumped furiously to keep her out of the watery grave waiting below.

A shrill cry pierced her ears. Turning her head in the direction of the sound, she swam with a few frenzied strokes toward the two heads bobbing up and down. Her limbs quickly succumbed to the ice-cold temperatures, but she knew she had to reach them before the elderly woman and child sank beneath the water. Her hand brushed against the woman's dress, the water-soaked material swishing like silk over her skin. She stopped swimming and furiously pedaled her feet in the water like she'd learned to do as a child. The woman looked ancient, her face scrunched into a mass of wrinkles. Glazed obsidian eyes speared her own, their silent message clearly understood.

Sophia had only been in the water a few minutes, but she was already exhausted. She reached forward, trying to grab hold of them both, but the woman shoved the child in her direction and Sophia's arm automatically wrapped around the wriggling body. As tiny hands grabbed hold of her neck, the old woman sank beneath the frigid water. The child crawled up her body, holding on to her neck with a death grip. She cradled the little one with one arm while her other pulled back and forth through the water, struggling to keep them afloat.

Glancing over her shoulder, she saw the boat as the giant vessel slowly cut through the water. She was running out of time. She scissored her tired legs and thrust out with her one free arm when something hit the water nearby. She bit back a scream when an arm snaked around her waist.

Relief washed through her when Clay's voice shouted in her ear, "Just hold onto the boy—I'll do the swimming!" She tightened her grip around the frightened child and held him as tightly as she could with her numb arms. "Th-th-thank y-you!" she yelled, grateful Clay had shown up when he had. Shaking violently, her teeth chattering, she fought the thick darkness clouding her vision.

Through half-closed eyes, she tried to focus on the painted planks as someone pulled her over the side of the boat and into Martin's outstretched arms. She couldn't feel her body anymore, and her mind wouldn't work. She whimpered as several of the women rubbed her arms and legs with old blankets, making her skin feel as if they were peeling it from her bones.

Clay's anxious face appeared above hers. Without saying a word, he pulled her up into his tight embrace and warmed her lips with a kiss. She was amazed at the gentleness of his kiss compared to the vise-like grip he had on her body. *Too bad I can't feel my lips,* she thought before slipping into a dreamless sleep.

CHAPTER 7

Clay's arms wrapped around her sodden form, holding on to Sophia as firmly as he could without hurting her. As he sat on the ship's deck holding her, the child crawled into her lap and promptly fell asleep. They'd wrapped blankets around him as well, but they all needed to get the wet clothes off before they succumbed to hypothermia.

A hard shudder tore through him when he realized how close she'd come to dying. Somehow, during the last month, this tiny but incredibly strong woman had wormed her way into his heart. He sat in stunned silence, staring down at her beautiful face. Silky black hair framed her skin—a rich, dark cream, and perfect. His chest felt hot and swollen as a powerful emotion extinguished the doubts and disbeliefs. He loved her.

He wanted to scream at the heavens. Nothing and no one, not even the woman he loved, was going to stop him from avenging his family. That vow would always come first.

As the hours passed, Martin's and Clay's anxiety increased.

"Sophia? *Aiukli*? You need to wake up now," Clay's voice broke. He'd talked to her constantly since she'd gone limp in his arms, hoping she would hear him calling to her. She'd been unconscious for almost eight hours, and pushing back the growing panic gripping his chest was getting harder to do by the minute. Taking turns with Martin, they both held her and tried to warm her icy skin, and it helped. Somewhat. The child also slept, tightly wrapped in her arms.

Clay caught Martin's steady gaze, and for the hundredth time asked, "She will be fine, right?"

Martin nodded once. His eyes narrowed but never left her pale face. Clay waited while the older man worked out whatever was bothering him.

Martin cleared his throat a couple of times. "I heard you talking…just before she rescued the little one." Clay watched the emotions play across Martin's tight face. He'd never seen his father's friend so bothered about anything but kept his mouth shut and waited for Martin to continue.

"Did I ever tell you about my daughter?" he asked in a tired voice. Clay shook his head. He vaguely remembered hearing his father speak about her, but she'd died when Clay was young, so he hadn't paid much attention.

"My Water Lily was beautiful, and so much like her mother. The earth was happy when she smiled. We still lived together as a tribe while she grew up, but by the time Water Lily had grown into a woman, most tribe members had moved off to their own farms." Martin paused, and Clay noticed the faraway glint in the old man's eyes. He could almost see the lifetime of memories as they tumbled over one another in their depths. Sophia's body twitched, pulling his gaze back down to her beautiful face.

"One day, Water Lily found an injured white man with a badly broken leg. Afraid he would die from infection if left alone, she brought him to our home. Under her healing touch, the man grew strong, and they fell in love. Almost one year later, they had a child of their own. A beautiful daughter. My Klara and I never knew such peace. Just after Rain Blossom turned one, Water Lily took her to Savannah and gave our granddaughter to a white family for them to raise as their own. Water Lily died soon after without telling us who they were. Her husband, Jerrod, returned from his month-long trip to find his wife dead and his daughter gone. He was devastated." Martin's red eyes moved from Sophia's face to stare out across the ship's deck. "We never found our Rain Blossom. In less than one week, we lost all three."

A band tightened across Clay's chest as the old man's pain became his. He knew what being alone was like—a hollowness deep inside that nothing could fill. He looked down at the beauty in his lap. *Until her.* An idea crept into his mind as he mulled over what he'd just learned. "How did Water Lily know she was dying? Could she have been worried about what the Cherokee would do with Rain Blossom after she was gone?"

Martin shrugged. "I don't know how she knew, or what she was thinking. We would never have turned either one away. Jerrod had become one of us—he was Cherokee in all ways but skin."

"I don't think she believed what anyone told her. It's the only thing that makes sense. Certain Choctaw tribes, for instance, follow the same rule—if the child's father is white and the mother dies, they are sent away from the tribe." He readjusted his cramped position on the deck's hard wood surface, careful not to waken Sophia, and wished the boat could travel faster through the ice-packed river. With the normal crossing still closed, the captain had traveled further south in order to get them safely across. He pulled Sophia closer as another gust of wind seared into his skin, freezing him to the bone. He could only hope she was warm enough.

"I don't remember seeing a white man in your home when father and I visited."

"He was only there for those two years. Through a friend, I heard he might have joined the army. Several years later, the same friend told us he was seen at the docks, but disappeared again. I haven't heard anything since. It has long puzzled me. This was not the same man who loved my Water Lily. The man I knew would never have left his daughter in someone else's home. The day he left, he promised me he would find our Rain Blossom and bring her home."

A great, deep *croak, croak, croak* came from the water, drawing his gaze. Several large, majestic birds glided over the water to the river's edge, while one flew through the air near the boat. The beautiful pelican floated, intently watching something just beneath the river's surface. Suddenly, his head dropped, skimming the surface and then drawing both water and food into the flat orange bill. Where the bottom of the bill met the bird's snowy white neck, a pouch-like orange membrane had expanded with the scooped water that now drained out again. When the water was all gone, the pouch had shrunk back to its normal size. The bird flipped its head a couple of times, swallowed the fish, and then started the process over again. After eating his fill, the elegant pelican flapped his long wings and gracefully soared back into the bright blue sky.

Clay glanced down as Sophia moved her head. Hope flared, and his mouth moved into a sly grin as an idea formed.

Martin's voice broke through his reverie. "What are you grinning at?"

"Life."

Martin harrumphed. "That's almost positive, coming from you."

"I also thought of a plan to keep our girl here safe."

For the first time since his wife died, Martin truly smiled. As Clay quickly related the details of his plan, the elder man's smile widened.

"What have I missed? You both look entirely too happy."

Clay's heart felt like it had burst, sending white-hot warmth through him. He held back the urge to pull her close and kiss her. Instead, he continued to hold her as he had for the past nine hours.

Martin's gnarled fingers smoothed her tangled mass of ebony hair, tucking it behind one ear. "You scared me, Granddaughter." Martin gently wiped her cheek with the back of his large hand. "You also made an old man proud."

Clay held out several pieces of dried jerky, chuckling as she stuffed most of one thick piece into her mouth. "And Martin didn't think you'd like it."

"Zoh guhd." She rolled her eyes in bliss.

Clay watched a tiny hand tug on her sleeve, pulling her gaze down to her side. An amazing look of wonder washed over her beautiful face as she gazed at the little boy she'd risked her life to save.

Lifting her head, Sophia caught sight of two large, dark-brown eyes staring at her from a scared little face. All the frantic emotions and adrenaline from her frozen swim rushed back. She couldn't stop herself from pulling the child up into her shaky embrace. "Ohhhh," she breathed and rested her chin on top of his warm head. "I did it. I saved him."

Clay leaned forward and rewrapped the double layer of blankets around them as best he could. "Yes you did, *aiukli*. However foolish a move it was, you saved the boy."

A shutter came down over his face, and she wondered what had just happened. "I couldn't let them die." She pinched her lips together then sighed. "The woman was so old. How did she float for so long? The water was freezing."

Her eyes filled, but the crystalline liquid only pooled in the bottom crescents. "Why did she give up?"

"She was old and had lived a full life." Martin's eyes glittered, but any sadness was replaced by humor. "I'd known that woman for many years. She was as playful as a sprite, and the Cherokee people will honor her sacrifice. Could she do anything less for her grandson?"

Sophia closed her eyes tightly. "Now I feel worse."

"Because you tried?" he argued. "You risked your own life to save theirs. Reverend Bushyhead is a fine man and a good leader. He will honor the life of his sister for what she did. Her sacrifice was one of love, Sophia. Honor her strength and yours. Because of you both, the little one is alive."

She took a deep breath, her fingers gently combing through the boy's tangled hair. Her thoughts tumbled over each other as she tried to calm her shaky nerves. As the minutes ticked by, she realized it wasn't working. Her nerves were now more jumbled than her thoughts. Clay's thumb rubbing the tender skin under her ear wasn't helping either, especially since she was still lying in his lap. And enjoying every second.

Her inner destruction was interrupted by the child's pitiful cry. "*E do da?* Papa?" the boy asked in a pathetic whimper.

Her grip tightened, hugging him close to her warm chest. "Everything will be all right, sweeting." Her gaze fell on her doll, lying close to Martin's crossed legs, and pointed to it. He handed her the doll, which she held it in front of the small boy. Her lips curled into a smile when his tiny fingers brushed over the painted face, and Sophia placed her in his chubby little arms. They all smiled when he curled up against her and laid his pink cheek against the doll's head for comfort.

"I promise we will find your papa as soon as we get off

the boat." *I hope.* Keeping her voice soft, her captivating whispers calmed him until his little eyes slid closed, and he fell into an agitated sleep.

SOPHIA PULLED her empty arms around her waist, missing the little boy's tiny grip as his father carried him away. She'd known the minute the ships docked and they disembarked, the child's family would be waiting for him to appear. He'd only been with her for a couple of days, but his sweetness had wrapped around her heart. The relief and love she'd seen on the father's face when he saw his son had made the sadness of saying goodbye a little bit easier to deal with.

CHAPTER 8

A warm breeze skipped over Sophia's skin, and spring blossomed everywhere she looked. In the day's fading warmth as the sun sent, she saw hundreds of small green buds covering the trees that hadn't been there the day before. A few sentinels stood out amongst all the color, their branches bare in testament to the hard winter. She hoped the dead-looking trees were only late bloomers. All around them, colors blazed with the excitement of new life. Soft yellows and pinks of unknown plants peeked out from among dark oranges and blues as the wild foliage began its spring growth.

The land, so close to her new home, was beautiful. After breathing in the frigid winter for so long, the warmth of spring and the fresh air laden with hints of honeysuckle and pine tickled her nose. Even with the small patches of icy snow still splattered across the landscape in every direction, chirping birds created a musical symphony that pushed the empty wintry silence away. She could only hope the emergence of new life would give her reprieve from the horrible memories that had plagued her since she'd been abducted.

Martin edged forward, and she slowed to match his shuffling steps. "How are you feeling?" she asked, glad that he'd regained a bit of color in his cheeks. Even his eyes held a sparkle that had been absent since leaving Georgia.

"Bryan said to make camp here." Martin tugged once on her arm, then turned and walked back to the wagon that had stopped a few feet behind them.

Emotionally exhausted, she didn't want to eat. Instead, she crawled into the back of the wagon and curled up in the corner. She tried to cover what she could of herself with the blanket's tattered remains, but finally gave up and threw the useless cover over her legs. She held up the doll and looked at its dirty face, rubbing most of the dust off with her thumb. She sighed and placed the doll back in the crook of her arm.

"Clay said we should arrive at our new home tomorrow," she whispered to the surrounding silence. "If the weather behaves, that is. I don't mind walking in the rain, I just don't want to see another river for a while. I wish I could see the future so I could know what is going to happen." She frowned as thoughts of her past flashed through her mind. "On second thought, maybe not. I don't want to know if it's something bad. At least until it happens, I can be blissfully ignorant and happy." She twirled the doll's hair around a finger. "If I'm honest with myself, I can admit to being scared of ending up alone."

She glanced at the doll's sightless eyes. "This morning, Martin asked me to live with him. I feel as if I've known him my entire life." Closing her eyes, she let her thoughts wander, and her mind drifted like a slow-moving stream, lazily winding and twisting around sandy bends and rocky outcroppings until the current picked up, and she found herself plunging over a waterfall and crashing into the rocks below with one single thought.

Clay.

She turned over on her side and moved the doll from beneath her ribcage, drawing comfort from her only link to home. With one arm curled beneath her head, Sophia whispered into the toy's tiny ear.

"I love him so very much, but I don't dare tell him. My heart aches when I'm not near him, and hurts more when I am. The closer we get to the Territory, the angrier he gets. Not so much in his words or actions, but in his eyes—and he won't tell me what's wrong." She sniffed in aggravation, and her thoughts darkened. "I'm also tired of worrying about Major Todd." She held the doll in front of her face and pursed her lips. "I don't think I want much from life—family, friends, and someone to love me as much as I love him." She hugged the doll to her again in frustration. "No, it's not too much to ask for."

Her eyelids slowly lowered, only to fly open again when her body jerked. She listened to the nightly noises of the settling camp, now so familiar and comforting. Her eyes closed again. Her last thought as she fell asleep was Clay's handsome face.

Clay knew he was hurting Sophia, but he couldn't seem to stop himself. He'd been alone for so long, he wasn't sure he knew how to share his life with someone else. His mind warred with the stupid organ pounding in his chest. For his own sanity, as well as to honor the vow he'd made to his family, he knew he had to leave…and soon. If he didn't, he'd never be strong to walk away from her. The one constant in his life had always been his nightmares. After the river, though, they'd changed. He would find his family, lying together, their vacant, unseeing eyes staring up into the sky. Then the dream morphed and Sophia joined them, her beautiful brown eyes closed in death. Both waking and sleeping, he saw Sophia jumping off the boat into the frozen river and he couldn't get to her in time to stop her. The thought of her dying disturbed him more than he wanted to admit. He absently rubbed his chest, trying to massage away the sharp pain that never seemed to go away.

He'd talk to Martin. Maybe if they put their heads together, he would find his answer.

Voices edged into Sophia's dreams, shifting her thoughts from fun-filled days and innocence to more mature, pressing issues. She recognized both Martin's and Clay's voices, but when a third deep voice began to argue, she woke up completely. Bryan was back. She hadn't seen him in more than a week, which had worried her. Major Todd was a harsh taskmaster and was never satisfied with anything any one person did, especially the soldiers serving under him.

She yawned, her mouth opening so wide she thought her jaws would pop apart. Her whole body shook with the effort. Stretching the sleep and fatigue from her body, she tuned in on their conversation.

"Major Todd decided this? Even more Cherokee will die if they aren't given food." Clay's words were clipped, and his voice sounded angry and dangerous. Drawing shallow breaths, she was able to hear what they said easier…she just had to hope she wouldn't hyperventilate from the effort.

"I know," Bryan said. "A few of us stole as much food as we dared from the supply wagons."

For a few seconds, the only sounds came from the nearby evergreens, as cicadas chirped their song to the last light of the day. As the silence continued, she wondered if their conversation had ended until she heard Clay's voice again.

"Bryan, we need your help watching over her. This morning, I overheard two soldiers laughing about how Todd was bragging, telling the men that nothing will stop him from taking her."

"And we know the *her* he's talking about," Martin's gravelly voice added.

Sophia scrambled to the ground. If she hadn't been in such a panic, she would have been embarrassed when she fell to her knees between the two men. Clay's hand reached out to steady her as he automatically pulled her to his side, his hand wrapping around the back of her neck and gently squeezing. Her skin burned under his touch as fiery tingles raced across her shoulders. The man had magic fingers as he gently massaged away the painful knots.

She took a calming breath. "What has Major Todd said about me?" She fidgeted with a crease in Clay's trousers—unmindful of his squirming—while she waited for someone to respond. When no one did, she glanced around to where she supposed the other two men were sitting, but in the moonless night, she couldn't see anything. "Please. Somebody tell me. I have a right to know."

She heard the scratching of skin on skin beside her and knew Clay scrubbed his face with his other hand. "You're right. This is about you...maybe if you understood what we're trying to do, you'll be safer."

The gentle caressing motion of her hand on his leg stopped, her fingers digging into the rough material. "Is it truly that bad?"

He dropped his arm down her back, his hand resting against her hip. "You don't need to hear his exact words, but you will understand their meaning." Clay's voice hardened. "He will do anything to have you, but we're not going to let that happen, Sophia. *I* will not let that happen."

She leaned into him as both shock and even a tiny bit of excitement flooded through her. The importance of his explanation was temporarily shoved aside as she concentrated on one word. He'd said *I.* Her heart raced. He wasn't going to let anything happen to her. *Does that mean he truly cares for me?* Truly, she'd never felt more safe, or loved.

On her other side, Martin cleared his throat, which seemed to echo in the night's silence, jolted her from her wayward thoughts. "You cannot be alone. Ever. It is just a matter of time, but Todd will come after you," Martin said. "Never let down your guard. You must pay attention to everything going on around you."

"If all three of you think this is absolutely necessary..." Her voice disappeared, drowned out by a rattling noise somewhere in the darkness. Not being able to see their expressions made her uncomfortable.

The rattling noise drew closer. The tension in the air around her increased. Her stomach's jittery dance grew wilder. A cricket's lonely chatter sounded close by, the sound grating on her already frayed nerves. Holding her breath didn't help either, because she then heard the harsh *thud, thud, thud* of her heartbeat echo loudly in her ears. A boot scraped the hard ground, and the cricket's song stopped. When something touched her ear, she couldn't squelch the high-pitched squeal fast enough.

Bryan chuckled. "Sorry."

Her hand flew out and luckily hit his shoulder and not his face. "*Ohhhh*. You scared me to death!" She glared at the faint outline of his head. Even though her eyes had become accustomed to the darkness, she could still barely make out the hazy outlines of everything around her. "I never even knew you'd left." The last thing she wanted to do was admit to him that she wasn't paying attention when that was the very thing they'd just been telling her to do.

"You found out something more?" Clay scooted the two of them over and made room for Bryan to sit.

"I went scoutin'. I like knowin' where everyone is. Todd is one campsite behind you."

"Damn," Clay mumbled. "He's too close. We don't need that."

"Well, you'll like this even less. As I walked by, I heard two officers complainin' about what he's doing. Said it was too much like cowardice. They think he should just take Miss Sophia if he wants her so bad."

Martin's growl echoed in her ear, and she reached over and squeezed his hand. The night was so still and quiet, she heard Bryan's intake of air before he spoke. "I'm only repeating their stupidity. There are just as many soldiers who think he should leave well enough alone. There are at least ten soldiers watchin' over you. Unfortunately, the major has more, and I don't know everyone here."

Clay swore, his grip tightening painfully on her hip. "That's not what we needed to hear."

"Thank you. Now I will never get to sleep." Fed up with the whole situation, and disgusted with herself for ever talking to the major in the first place, she stood. "I don't want to hear anymore. I will be in the wagon counting the stars. Goodnight." She edged toward what she hoped was the wagon, thankful when her fingers brushed over the rough wood. She crawled back up to her previous spot and laid down.

Tucking one arm under her head for a pillow, she wrapped the other around her doll and pulled the hard little body against her own. Sophia rested her lips against the doll's coarse hair. Ignoring the tickle, she whispered, "I'm so tired of being scared," ignoring the slight tickle of hair against her lips. She drew the crisp air deep into her lungs and knew falling back asleep after what she'd just learned would be impossible.

CHAPTER 9

Clay was thankful Sophia had returned to the wagon. Now they could talk freely without scaring her more than she already was. "There's no need for you to be defensive, Bryan. No one is accusing you of anything." Clay leaned toward the younger man. "The closer we get to the Territory, the less I trust Todd. He's going to try something before then, and we will need to be prepared."

"I'm doing everything I can!" Bryan said, exasperation behind every word.

Clay felt Martin's heavy hand cover his knee. "Bryan will do right by our Sophia. He's taken good care of us since this dreadful journey began, and being this close to the end won't change that."

In the night's blackness, he heard Bryan's shaky intake of air, but Clay couldn't stop the building sense of urgency and reached out, grabbing the soldier's upper arm. "Guard her with your life."

"I already do, sir." Bryan's threw back his shoulders, jerking his arm from Clay's grip. His chin rose as he stared back at Clay. "Miss Sophia has given more to these people, and me, than she will ever know. Her caring and positivity throughout this horrifying ordeal has given everyone hope when there hasn't been any. Where the government works to bend the Indians' backs and change their beliefs, Miss Sophia allows them to stand tall and proud, and keeps the Cherokee ways alive by asking questions and learning about their culture. Miss Sophia has made me a better soldier and a better man." He turned to walk away, then stopped, his boot sliding over the loose scree. "I discovered the names of the men you've been searching for. The ones who killed your family." Bryan leaned closer and whispered the two names then walked away.

Clay let him go and rested the back of his head against the wagon's wheel as he replayed the entire conversation with Bryan. It seemed Sophia had not only made an impression on him, but also on the young soldier. And if Bryan's short speech was to be believed, the entire tribe as well. Plus, he now had the information he needed to fulfill his vow. He stretched out his legs and crossed his arms over his chest. From the loud pops next to him, mixed with a couple of grunts, he could tell Martin had just stood up.

"I believe I will follow Sophia's example and go to bed now. You should try to get a little sleep." Martin grunted a few more times. "I'm old, so you must listen to me."

Clay listened as Martin made his way to the wagon, a grin lifting one side of his mouth. He squirmed on the hard-packed ground in a futile attempt to find a smooth spot, but the hard, pebbly surface just dug into his behind.

Time passed slowly for Clay, the information that Bryan gave him keeping him awake. He stared into the swirls of inky blue dotted here and there with clusters of winking white crystals across the horizon.

The outer edges of the heavens were just beginning to lighten as dawn closed in. He should have been asleep for hours already, but his brain wouldn't shut down. He stretched his arms out and rolled his shoulders, trying to relieve some of the cramped tenseness that had plagued him since Martin had gone to bed.

He thought back to his youth, before the lonely years following his family's death. He still felt his mother's loving touch as she soothed away his numerous aches and pains, and the thrill of catching his first fish with his father. His favorite memory, though, was the birth of his beautiful little sister.

Knowing he wouldn't be getting any sleep that night, Clay shook off the memories and stood. Muttering under his breath, he marched to the end of the wagon. He kept his touch soft and laid his hand on Martin's leg, biting back laughter when the old man jerked upright, eyes wide and bright.

"What is it?" Martin hissed.

Clay leaned forward. "I'm leaving." He held up his hand before Martin could object. "Thanks to Bryan, I finally have *something*. He gave me their names, Martin. I have to finish this before I can move on." Clay could finally honor the promise he'd made to his parents after so many years of failure.

Martin stared at him, unblinking. He held so still, Clay wondered if he'd fallen asleep with his eyes open. Finally, a long sigh escaped through Martin's closed lips, and his shoulders slumped forward. "You will find them, Nighthawk—when it is time. They will still be out there if you stay. I am no longer a young man, and you are needed here. Sophia needs you. You promised her protection. That, too, is a vow."

The tumbling stones in Clay's stomach multiplied. He swallowed the bile as it burned a path up his throat, the fight to stay almost winning. He couldn't tell Martin that Sophia was a large part of his decision to go. After their kiss on the boat, he realized just how much he loved her…and therein was the problem. He had to leave now, or he never would.

His gaze dropped to her perfect face. A few dark strands of hair teased her cheek and upper arm as the cool morning breeze played tug-of-war with each strand. Her lashes formed black crescents against her pale cheeks. Even asleep, she twisted his heart. A crooked grin curved his lips as he stared at her mouth. *She sleeps with her mouth open.*

His eyes traced the classic lines of her face and long neck. He'd failed to notice how prominent her cheekbones had become, and shoved the niggling worry from his mind. He drank her in, and couldn't help but wonder if it would be the last time.

"*Humph.* You are running away, Nighthawk. Chasing those men is only an excuse. You run away from life." Clay met the old man's hard gaze. "Go. Before she wakes. I will tell her something," Martin snarled.

Surprised at the vehemence in his friend's voice and the disgust on his face, Clay's only response was a quick nod. He turned on his heel and quickly strode toward a nearby grove of trees, where Bryan had said a horse would be waiting. Luckily, his young friend had also taken care of the guards, at least long enough for him to slip away.

He inched up to the sturdy-looking blue roan, holding out an open palm and speaking in soft, soothing tones to gain the animal's confidence. As the morning sun crested on the eastern horizon, the blues turned to purples and a tapestry of soft, pale colors wove through the sky. He threw a leg over the saddle and turned the horse's head without a backward glance. In the dense canopy above, the melodious tunes from several mourning doves went unnoticed as he absently rubbed the aching spot over his heart.

CHAPTER 10

From his vantage point behind the heavy foliage growing along the tree line, the major watched as the old Indian stared into the empty wagon. One corner of the major's mouth tipped up in the semblance of a smile, and an almost satisfied feeling settled in his midsection. Almost. He wouldn't be completely happy until that dratted female was taken care of, one way or another.

His gaze followed the movement of the young soldier as he hurried toward the wagon. Todd recognized him as the upstart who'd caused such a ruckus about what the dirty heathens deserved. Well, he was an officer in the United States Army, and he was not about to deprive his men of three good meals a day. They worked hard and deserved whatever he could give them—at least until he decided otherwise.

Major Todd stepped back into the shadows of the trees and raised the field glasses to his eyes. He wanted to see the devastation on the old man's face, knowing he wouldn't be able to do anything to help Sophia. Especially since they would never find her in time. She was already an hour away from here, tucked away in the back of his wagon. He'd have to hurry to catch up, but he simply couldn't miss their reaction to finding her gone.

The young soldier, whatever his name was, leaned forward and rested one hand on the old man's shoulder. The major couldn't hear what the soldier said to the old Indian, but that didn't matter. He chuckled when the old man seemed to shrink in stature. His head fell forward to rest against the crook of his elbow, which rested on top of the wagon's side wall. A fullness expanded in the major's chest when the soldier turned heel and left the Indian wallowing in his apparent sorrow.

Content that his plan was working, Todd made his way through the small grove of trees to where he'd left his horse. He mounted, and with a hard jerk of the reins, he galloped away from the large camp. After several miles and no one on his trail, he rammed the heels of his boots into the gelding's tender sides, spurring the horse into a full run. There was no more time to waste. He had a young lady to call upon, and a plan to finish.

CHAPTER 11

*S*eeing Martin and Bryan ahead of him, Clay relaxed for the first time since making his second getaway from the soldiers. His horse slowed as it caught up to the two men and stopped, both man and animal dragging much-needed air into their deprived lungs. He knew pushing the animal wasn't smart, but the building fear pounding through him erased all reason. During the frantic ride to catch up with Martin and Bryan, he'd blamed himself. *If only he'd stayed and protected her as he'd promised.* By leaving camp, he'd all but handed Sophia to Todd.

"Clay?" Strain was evident in Martin's weak voice.

Winded, Clay held up his hand, trying to slow his breathing. "You were right, Martin. I was running away. I was almost to the border between Arkansas and the Territory and realized I couldn't leave her, so I returned to camp." He sucked in a large breath. "The boy Sophia saved—his father told me what happened, and that you and Bryan had gone after her. This is all my fault. If I hadn't left…"

Martin shook his head. "Blaming yourself won't help Sophia." One bushy gray brow rose. "And neither will killing a perfectly good horse. We expected this, Clay. Just not today."

"But if I'd stayed…"

"He would've found another way," Bryan interrupted. "We need to figure out where he's taken her, not who's at fault."

Clay studied the younger man, one brow raised high on his forehead. "How did you manage to get away?"

Bryan gave him a crooked grin. "One of the soldiers owed me a favor and helped me hide the horses. When it was my turn to keep watch, I woke up Martin and we left. They should be realizing about now that a horse is missing and I'm not there."

Martin's eyes narrowed thoughtfully at Clay. The old man leaned forward, resting his crossed arms over the pommel of his saddle. "The Choctaw settlement's south of here. Have either of you ever traveled up this way?"

Clay nodded. "I have, but there's nothing around here…" He chewed on the inside of his cheek, trying to remember the terrain and where the major might take Sophia. "If I remember correctly, there are ancient burial mounds not too far from here. Celebrations and burials are still held there by some of the smaller tribes in the area." He saw the flicker of hope in Martin's eyes.

Bryan walked his gelding forward a few paces. "I know the place you're talkin' about. My grandfather lives close to Fort Smith. He's Cadodacho. He's taken me to Spiro for the fall busk every year since I was old enough to walk. The busk is a celebration of my people."

Clay stared at him with a quizzical expression on his face. "You're Indian? How in the hell are you serving in the army?"

Bryan's horse struck the ground a couple of times with its hoof. "Dad's Irish," he explained with a widening grin. "I got into the army 'cuz I favored him." He shrugged. "Guess I never got around to tellin' the Army about the rest of my family."

Martin chuckled, nodding with approval. "You are a surprising young man, Bryan MacConnell. I like that. We have mounds like your Spiro back home. It is a spiritual place. Sacred." He turned to look at Clay then glanced back at Bryan. "How far to these mounds?"

Bryan thought a moment. "Two, maybe three miles."

Martin grinned. "Well then, what are we waiting for? Lead the way."

Sophia's face hurt something awful. She tried to open her mouth, but something prevented her from being able to... and whatever it was tasted foul. Her fingers felt along the strands of rope that tied her hands together. Examining the knot, she knew she wouldn't be able to undo it without help. She tried to move her feet and found that they, too, had been bound. As she began to realize something was very, very wrong, her breathing quickened, but something heavy weighed on her chest and made breathing difficult.

Reaching over to her left, she felt rough wood. She found the same on her right and realized she was in the bed of a wagon with a canvas tarp covering the top. The rocking, side-to-side motion as the wheels maneuvered over the uneven land calmed her nerves. Her frantic breathing slowly evened out, and she began to notice other things. She wrinkled her nose in disgust as a sour stench filled her nostrils.

Time crept by as she lay in the enclosed bed. Unable to move or see anything other than the dim light of the sun as it soaked through the canvas, the panic she'd initially felt had long since disappeared, changing to tediousness. Her entire body ached, her muscles cramping from the tight bindings around her wrists and ankles.

She slowly inhaled the stale air surrounding her as it heated with the afternoon sun. For the hundredth time, she flexed her arm and leg muscles without hope of regaining any feeling. Every now and then, two voices mumbled somewhere in front of her, and then the oppressive silence closed in again. It went on hour after hour until she thought she would go crazy.

Even after listening to the two men all day, she still had no idea where they were taking her. An awful feeling of dread washed over her when the voice closest to her spit out several hard, clipped words, disgust evident in his harsh tone. Unfortunately, she knew that voice all too well, and her worst fear had come true. Major Todd had finally succeeded in capturing her.

She closed her eyes with a groan. She was in grave danger. Her only hope of rescue was if someone back at camp had seen or heard something…but since the wagon was rolling on at a leisurely rate, she highly doubted anyone had.

She replayed the previous night's events and tried to fill in the blanks. She remembered angrily stomping to the wagon. She had fallen asleep, dreaming about her childhood, and the next thing she remembered were strong arms jerking her from the wagon. There hadn't even been time for a loud scream. Struggling had only infuriated her captor, and when her foot struck him, something hard and heavy slammed into the side of her head. She didn't remember anything after that until waking up and realizing she was a prisoner.

"Captain Johnson," Major Todd said, his disgusted tone interrupting Sophia's thoughts. "Stop blabbering and simply tell me the location of the camp…if you can manage to think with that tiny brain of yours."

"Major, the final relocation camp is over that hill up yonder. Can you see those two pines ahead? Those tall ones?

The turnoff to get to the camp is just before that and will take us to the mounds."

"How long?"

"'Nother hour, I reckon."

"That will be all, Captain. Report back to camp."

"Yessir."

Listening to Todd's off-key whistling worsened the throbbing in her head until she had a full-blown headache. Unfortunately, when he stopped whistling, the droning of his unpleasant, whiny voice took over. After a while, she stopped paying attention to what he said, her single focus on undoing the knotted rope encircling her wrists. She forced her bloodless fingers to work at the knot, hoping to at least loosen it before they reached their destination.

After a while, no matter how hard she tried, she couldn't tune out the major's rambling. The longer she listened, however, the more horrified she became when she realized what she was hearing. She finally knew what he was going to do to her. He wasn't taking her because he wanted a wife. He was going to kill her.

The canvas tarp above her was suddenly ripped away from the wagon with a *whoosh,* and Sophia was jerked from the bed, hitting the ground with a hard thud and a very unladylike grunt. Her hip and elbow burned from scraping along the rocky soil. She turned her glare to the man who'd caused all of her troubles over the last eight months.

With her hands still tied behind her, sitting up was harder than she expected, but she wouldn't give Major Todd the satisfaction of helping her do anything. She kicked her bound feet at him. "*Ay eeyl keyoo!*" she screamed, but with her teeth chewing against the bridle of cloth tied around her head, the words were unintelligible. Major Todd only laughed and grabbed several things from the wagon's seat and walked away.

Sophia stared up at the sky. The day was gone, and soft shades of red and orange streamed through the darkening blue-gray expanse overhead. From the corner of her eye, she watched every move the major made as he set up their camp. She had one, maybe two hours of daylight left to figure out how to get away from the madman.

She tensed when he dropped the last branch onto the small fire he'd built then turned and headed in her direction. His boots crunched and scuffled across the pebbly ground. Concentrating on the sky, she drew in what little air she could as her lungs quivered like jelly inside her chest. Fear pounded in her head.

"Since you sat here like a good girl, I will let you sit with me and eat." He knelt and grabbed her chin, his nails biting painfully into her cheek as he lifted her face. "However, should you scream, I will return the gag. It might be best if you don't talk at all." He jerked at the knot, and the disgusting cloth cut into the edges of her mouth.

She pressed her lips together to relieve their stinging stretch, the metallic taste of blood coating her tongue. He jerked her upright, pulling hard on her arm. Trying to get moisture back into her parched, gritty mouth without water proved impossible, so she gave up and simply grunted, jerking her arm from Todd's grasp. Her glare never faltered. She concentrated on her hatred of him to take her mind off her sore shoulder and every other scraped and aching spot on her body.

Todd chuckled. "Good. Still full of spirit. I like that in a woman…until they take it too far." He motioned for her to follow him and pointed to an ancient-looking tree. Near the edge of its large overhanging canopy, a fire crackled and popped, the orange flames bouncing in and out of the thrown-together pile of logs.

Surprisingly, he gently eased her down onto the hard

ground in front of the comforting warmth and released the ropes from around her ankles. She stretched out her stiff legs as the blood returned to her limbs, tingling painfully. The major walked around the fire and sat, a haughty sneer pasted on his face. He'd left her hands tied together behind her.

The wonderful smell drifting to her nose from the pan resting on the burning logs made her stomach rumble. The last time she'd eaten a good meal seemed a lifetime ago, and the savory smell of roasting meat forced another, louder rumble from her shrunken stomach.

The major barked out a laugh. "Hungry?" He flipped the juicy meat, the fat popping as the raw side touched the hot surface, then caught her gaze with his. "You can have whatever is left over, but I can already tell you it won't be much. I'm hungry." She glowered at him as he practically preened at her in his pristine uniform. She glanced down at her own filthy appearance and grimaced. She couldn't wait to burn her dress, which was now little better than a cleaning rag.

"You know, dear Sophia, your young man is dead by now." He shrugged. "Or he soon will be." His words closed around her fragile heart and squeezed, their icy fingers sinking deep. Her mind screamed, but her lips remained clamped together. His eyes widened slightly. "What? No ranting or wailing? No crying? You aren't even going to beg for his life?" He raised a thin brow. "Hmmm, I'm disappointed."

"Why should I?" she asked, careful to keep her expression blank. "Pleading wouldn't do me any good. You can stop playing the charade. I know your real plan for me, and it isn't marriage."

His oily smile returned, sickening in its assurance. "No. But I would think you'd care just a tiny bit about what happens to your beau. As for the other? Well..."

She blinked, finding it almost impossible to keep her

facial muscles relaxed. "What do you mean? Mr. Clay Jefferson is merely a friend, nothing more." She was completely unprepared for the hurricane-force of anger that hurtled his slender body almost over the fire.

"You, then, are a strumpet! You kissed him! You kissed that dirty, red-skinned savage!" he spit out at her, his face growing redder with each passing second. "I refuse to allow my future wife to romp about with *those* people. Even if you are almost one of them…"

Her mind buzzed in confusion. "Excuse me?" Only a whisper pushed through her frozen lips as she tried to make sense of his words.

His condescending tone continued even after he marched back to the fire and flipped the browning meat again. "Emily assured me she had trained you to behave like a proper lady and not a half-breed. You are my property. I will simply have to kill him for touching you."

Sophia's skin turned clammy, and a million thoughts fluttered around her mind, but she couldn't think clearly. Could it be true? If it was true…that would mean she was part Indian. She sucked in air, holding it in her expanded lungs until they burned. It would explain so much in her life, especially why Emily Deveraux had treated her more like a servant than a daughter.

She knew Todd spoke the truth. That knowledge became a burning tidal wave of anger that filled her heart and mind at everything she'd had to endure from her mother, and the loss of what could have been with her real family. Her thoughts turned to Clay, and a fierce pleasure swelled her heart. She wasn't going to sit back like a fragile female and let anyone hurt him.

"You will not hurt him," she said in the harshest tone she could muster. He laughed and reached toward the pan sitting on the hissing fire with a wadded pad of material to wrap around the scalding handle. Sophia watched as a surge of orange flames shot toward him. Seeing an opportunity to escape, she raised her bound wrists and did the only thing her numb arms would allow her to do and hit the bottom of the pan, tossing the sizzling contents into his face. The chunk of meat, along with the hot grease, splattered over his face and hands. In morbid fascination, she watched his pasty skin turn brilliant red with a mask of white puffy blisters already covering the burned areas.

He scrambled to his feet, screaming and running around in a pain-filled frenzy. Suddenly, he turned and faced her, his eyes wild and accusing. "How dare you!" he screamed. He raced around the fire, and before she could move, grabbed her by the arm and dragged her across the uneven ground.

"You will pay for that, you filthy half-breed," he growled, shoving her into a dark hole near the base of a giant mound of dirt. Pushing her forward along the hole, he crawled in behind her, shoving and pushing her forward every time she faltered. Sophia's forehead slammed into the hard-packed earth again and again, her arms still not able to work properly.

Just when she thought she couldn't get any more scared, the chilling edge of his voice proved her wrong.

"It all makes sense!" he screamed behind her. "Why didn't I see it before, what you really are? You're a witch!" he screamed. "This is all a spell. A curse! Yes, that's it—that explains everything. From the moment I saw your face… you've controlled my actions…the very thoughts in my head."

Sophia rolled onto her back and listened in growing horror to his wild ramblings. She'd heard tales of witch hunts. The Salem trials had been almost a hundred and fifty years prior, but people still believed. She wanted to scream at him that she wasn't a witch, but she knew he wouldn't listen.

A shiver of apprehension rattled through her body as the cool underground air raised goose pimples on her skin.

She wasn't sure which of her options was the lesser evil. Major Todd was going to make sure she never left this horrible place. Inhaling the heavy, stagnant air, she knew she was running out of time.

"You don't deserve the life I would have given you." His reedy voice echoed within the small enclosure.

The smoldering ball of anger inside her chest exploded. "How many times do I have to tell you? I would *never* marry a man like you!"

"Now, dear Sophia, you aren't going to marry anyone." His voice faded away—along with his torchlight. The significance of his actions sank in, leaving a cold chill skittering down her spine. Fear churned in her stomach as she curled up and wrapped her arms around her knees, holding them to her chest. He'd actually left her in an underground, nameless place. And worse...she'd let him!

The deathly quiet closed in around her, pressing down until she couldn't breathe. However, before despair overwhelmed her, she stared as hard as she could at a lighter patch of darkness a few feet away. A small kernel of hope blossomed, and she rolled to one side. Using her elbow, she pushed hard against the ground and heard a *pop* then a loud *cra-ack* as something broke beneath her. Carefully moving her fingers over the dirt, she felt a sting as the pad of her finger sliced across the sharp edge of what felt like a piece of pottery.

In desperation, she sawed at the rope binding her wrists, thankful it wasn't very thick and they fell away without much effort. Drawing her feet underneath her, she tried to stand, but her head bumped against the low ceiling. Twisting around until she was on her knees, she crawled toward the small patch of light.

CHAPTER 12

Eastern Indian Territory

With as little noise as possible, Clay, Martin, and Bryan rode into the dark campsite. A dilapidated wagon lay with its long wooden tongue propped against the ground several yards away from the dying fire. Tied to the tongue was a lone gray horse, quietly pulling at tufts of grass between its hooves. Clay placed a finger against his lips and motioned for Martin and Bryan to dismount. They ground-tied their horses near the gray and cautiously spread out, finding good positions around the campfire.

The major's head was slumped forward, and as Clay crept closer, an occasional snore interrupted the silence. Clay's gaze, however, remained focused on the army-issue revolver gripped in the major's bandaged fist. Occasional bursts of red embers scattered into the night's gentle breeze. He stole a quick glance at the major's bright red face and wondered how the pathetic man in front of him had managed to work his way up the military chain of command.

Clay waited until he heard Bryan's quiet but distinctive

chirrup and Martin's *tur-a-lee,* telling him they were in place and ready. He continued forward and moved around the fire toward the slumbering man, halting when a loud *pop* from the fire echoed like a gunshot. The major's eyes flew open, and the gun rose, aimed at Clay's abdomen. The major scrambled to his feet, and the two men locked gazes in a venom-filled stare-down.

"Where is she, Todd?" Clay snarled. With a will of iron, he clamped down on the fury welling up inside his chest. He didn't like the out-of-control feeling—as if his heart had been cleaved in two—as the barely controlled anger roiled through him. He glanced over the large, oozing blisters covering Todd's face and hands, but bit back a humorless chuckle. *That's my girl. Gave him what he deserved, didn't you?*

"Have some trouble, Todd?" Clay knew the question hit a nerve when the major's hands twitched in time with his left eye.

"You are too late. Dear Sophia will die, just as you will, since you weren't smart enough to even bring a gun."

While the arrogant man boasted, Clay's hand inched behind his back, his fingers slowly curling around the handle of the knife he'd shoved behind his leather belt. With the familiar deer-horn gripped in his hand, he breathed a little easier.

A soft gasp sounded behind Clay, and time stopped. Todd jerked into motion and swung his pistol, his shot echoing in Clay's ear as Clay threw his knife. Todd's grip on the revolver slowly loosened as he stared at Clay in disbelief. His gaze fell to the knife protruding from his chest as the gun slipped through his nerveless fingers and landed with a dull *thud* on the ground. Several heartbeats passed before his body slithered downward, lifeless eyes staring up into the blinking night sky.

Clay whirled around, his mind tumbling over itself in fear

of what he would find. Martin lay on the ground with his head nestled in Sophia's lap, blood oozing from a hole in his shoulder. Relieved, he started toward them, only to twist back around when Bryan hollered at him from behind. Bryan pushed a newcomer into the campsite, his gun steady and aimed at the man's back.

Clay was surprised to see Sophia's strange little doll tucked into the crook of Bryan's arm. He tamped down his building frustration at not being able to help Sophia or Martin. Instead, Clay met the stranger's anxious gaze and addressed the man, his irritation visibly evident on his face.

"Who are you, and why are you here?" he demanded angrily.

The tall man stared into Clay's face. His dark brows lowered into a frown, as if trying to decide his options. Realizing he had none, he shrugged. "I'm camped on the other side of this strange place. I was minding my own business when I heard shouting. I scouted over this way, looking to see what was happening, and this fellow here," he said, tilting his head toward Bryan, "showed me his gun."

A small grunt sounded behind Clay, and he watched the stranger's mouth draw into a tight line. The man leaned sideways to see what was going on behind Clay. He took a step forward then jerked to a stop as Bryan jabbed him with the barrel of his gun. The man raised his hands in surrender. "You have someone hurt back there. I'm not a doctor, but I can do simple things." The man's anxious gaze traveled back and forth several times before finally resting on Clay's face. "Please," he pleaded. "Let me help."

"What's your name?"

"Santini. My name is Jerrod Santini."

Martin's weak voice rasped from behind them. "Jerrod? Is that really you?"

The stranger looked startled. Ignoring both Clay and

Bryan, he quickly moved toward Martin and kneeled at his side. Clay followed him and stopped next to Sophia. His gaze moved over her, noting the raw, red marks around her wrists. Other than those, she didn't seem to be injured. Despite the dirt and tear stains, she looked lovelier than she ever had.

He wanted nothing more than to pull her to him and hold her close, but he held himself back. Would she forgive him his stupidity? Before he was ready to know that answer, she looked up. His breath wedged against the lump clogging his throat as her tear-filled gaze met his.

Clay cleared his throat. "Are you all right?" His gaze dropped to her mouth. Her lips were chapped and her face was smudged with dirt, but to him, she was beautiful.

She watched the emotions fly across Clay's face and slowly nodded. "I was lucky. The major was too concerned about his burns and forgot to reseal the tunnel inside the mound. I crawled around until I found the inside opening, but when I was halfway through the tunnel, I heard voices." She took a step closer, wanting to wrap her arms around his waist and feel his heartbeat against her ear. He made her feel safe. Protected. "I knew you would find me," she said in a breathy whisper.

The tall, slim man knelt beside Martin, gripping the old man's gnarled hand in his own. "Martin? Is it really you? I came as soon as I heard about the forced moves. I'd almost given up hope of ever finding you and Klara." Jerrod moved Martin's shirt out of the way and studied the bleeding hole in the old Indian's shoulder. "What happened here? Who shot you?"

Martin coughed and waved off Jerrod's questions. "It's nothing. I'm fine." Martin reached his free hand out to lay it over Jerrod's. "Where have you been all these years? No one seemed to know where you disappeared to."

Jerrod threw a frantic glance toward Bryan, his face lined with anxiety. "Please?" he begged. "I need my saddlebag back at my camp. I have bandages and herbs that will help him."

Bryan met Clay's gaze and nodded in response to whatever he read in Clay's expression. Turning, he ran back into the woods and returned a few minutes later with the saddlebag. He dropped it on the ground next to Jerrod.

"Let me take care of your shoulder first, then we'll talk." Jerrod took the canteen from Bryan and poured the cool water over the seeping wound. He gently poked at the small hole, then gently raised the wounded man higher so he could examine the ragged edges of the exit hole in Martin's upper back.

"Well, you will live," Jerrod teased. "With most of the blood washed away, your injury isn't as bad as it first looked. The bullet went through your shoulder, so we won't have to dig it out. You know I need to clean the wound and make sure part of your shirt isn't in there." He pulled a small flask from the bag and poured the contents into the bullet hole front and back. Ignoring Martin's sharp intake of breath, Jerrod yanked out a folded handkerchief and pressed it against the wound to help staunch the flow of blood. Once it was more or less stopped, he shrugged out of his vest and fashioned it into a strange, workable sling.

Sophia sniffed back a quiet sob and gently touched the bandage. Still worried, she looked up, her thanks frozen on her lips as she met the man's stunned gaze. He raised his hand then dropped it back onto his knee without touching her. She squirmed when his steady gaze turned into frown. "Water Lily?" he asked in a hoarse whisper.

For a moment, she wondered if she'd heard him correctly. "What? No, I'm sorry. My name is Sophia."

Jerrod sat down heavily on the hard-packed ground. "You look so much like her—the same smile, the same sweet brown eyes a man could drown himself in." The man's face sagged, misery written in every line for the woman named Water Lily.

She leaned forward and laid her hand over his. "I am very sorry. Was Water Lily your wife?" He nodded. "What happened to her?" She waited while he pulled himself together, unaware of how silent everyone else had become.

"She died a long time ago, but I still miss her like it was yesterday. I never knew she was sick." He sighed. "I just couldn't accept that she was never coming back." He smiled sadly at Martin. "Martin and Klara took care of me—kept me from falling apart. When Water Lily left, she took our daughter somewhere, and I had to find her."

When Martin struggled to sit up, Sophia—with Clay's help—moved him closer to the wagon and let him rest against the wheel. She crisscrossed her legs, trying to squash her curiosity, wondering what it would feel like to be loved so completely by a man. She peered at Clay, but his stony face told her nothing. Could he love her the way Jerrod had loved his Water Lily?

Martin stared at Jerrod. "What became of you? You sent no word. We searched for you, but never found anything."

"I backtracked Water Lily and the baby all the way to Savannah, but then lost their trail. I found no trace of Rain Blossom at all. It was like my daughter had simply vanished."

Sophia frowned. "Why would your wife take your daughter away from you?"

Jerrod shook his head. "I have no idea. At first, I wondered if it was because I wasn't Cherokee. I couldn't help but think that had I stayed home and not gone away, she would have lived." He hung his head. "I'm sorry, Martin. I failed in my promise to you and Klara to find Rain Blossom and bring her home. By that time, I was too ashamed to return.

"I wandered through Savannah for a while, drowning my sorrow in a few taverns. It was in one of those that I ran into an old friend of mine. I was young and impressionable when Aaron took me under his wing. He taught me everything I needed to know about ships and sailing. He was like a father to me... Anyway, when we ran into each other, he offered me a job as his chief mate, and I accepted. But I never stopped looking for my family. After about twelve years, Aaron told me he wanted to spend more time with his daughter and offered me his ship, to run as her captain in his stead. I took her with mixed feelings. She's a good vessel, reliable, but at the same time she reminded me of what I had lost." He stared at the ground, breathing heavily. Finally, he raised his head. "The name of the ship is *Lily of the Sea*."

Sophia gasped, and the men turned to look at her. "No, that can't be."

"What is it, little one?" Martin reached for her but winced in pain at the movement.

"What was the name of this captain? The man you sailed with?" She pressed her hands against her stomach hoping to quell the jittering sensation building inside her.

Jerrod tilted his head, a question hovering on his tongue, but he answered her. "Aaron Deveraux. He was one of the best men I have ever known. I returned from a run to the Antilles only to discover that he and his wife had been murdered and their daughter missing. I didn't want to work for another man, so I left." He glanced at Martin. "I tried to find you and Klara, only to discover you'd been sent on this horrible march. I followed in the hopes of finding you. I finally gave up and decided to keep going west to see this new land where the government was sending the Indians."

Sophia pressed her hands to her mouth. Aaron Deveraux.

Her father. "It's true then, what Major Todd said." The words, strangled by her constricting throat, sounded raspy to her own ears. She tried to breathe around the heartache. "Aaron Deveraux was my father." She tried to smile. "And he *was* a good man." A tear streaked down her face, which she wiped away with the back of her hand and straightened her shoulders. She forced herself to look at Jerrod and was startled by the intensity of his gaze.

"You look so much like her...I don't understand. You said Captain Deveraux was your father?"

Sophia nodded, a warm flush filling her face, and she squirmed. "Yes."

"Forgive me, but you look nothing like him. Did you favor your mother?"

Surprised, she considered the question. Jerrod was right. Her father and mother had both been fair. Her heavy black hair and eyes were far different from theirs. "I...no, actually, I didn't." Martin and Jerrod exchanged a knowing look.

Her eyes narrowed. "What are you not telling me?"

"Could it be possible, Martin? All this time...practically under my nose?" The pain in Jerrod's voice tore at Sophia's heart. Her fist bunched in her skirt, but Martin reached over to pat her clenched fingers.

"I suspected she might be the first time I saw her," Martin said, his eyes on her. "You do, you know. You look like my daughter. You spoke of sailing with Captain Deveraux so often, Jerrod, of how much you admired him. I think Water Lily took Rain Blossom to him. I think she asked him to look after your child until you came for her, but he must have decided to keep the baby for himself." He smiled. "I would have done the same thing."

Sophia couldn't breathe. Emotions bubbled up from deep inside her until she thought she might explode. "I was adopted? That would explain why my mother hated me."

The admission flew out of her mouth before she could stop it.

"Did she hurt you?" Jerrod hissed.

Frightened by the intensity in his voice, she shook her head vehemently. "No, no. My parents—I mean, my adoptive parents—were good to me. Papa was very kind and truly loved me. Mama was...distant, but she never harmed me." She couldn't help but notice the pained expression that crossed Jerrod's face when she called Aaron Deveraux papa.

Reaching over, she touched her fingertips to the back of his hand. "I'm sorry. He was the man who raised me. But I would like the chance to get to know you." At that moment, the import of the whole situation burst upon her. Her eyes widened as she turned to Martin and tried to stifle her squeal of excitement. "But...that means you really *are* my grandfather!"

The old man smiled and patted her cheek. "You wrapped yourself around my heart from the moment we met. Now I understand what my heart has been telling me from the beginning, *u-we-tsi*. My granddaughter," he breathed.

Sophia glanced up and saw Bryan standing with something in his hands. "I found your doll in the wagon, Miss Sophia. I thought you might want it back," he said as he gave it to her.

She took the doll and held it tightly against her. "He was right."

Martin touched her shoulder. "Who was right, Granddaughter?"

She stared at the ground. "Papa...Mr. Deveraux. The night he gave her to me, he made me promise to always keep the doll with me. I thought his request strange, but he said the lady who gave him the doll insisted she wasn't just another plaything, but something special."

Jerrod reached over and touched the doll's chest where a

beautiful rose had been carved. The hint of a smile appeared. "My mother had a doll very much like this one when she was young. I haven't thought about that in years." He gave her a hesitant smile. "May I look at it a moment?"

Sophia nodded and handed it to him. She watched as he raised the doll's tattered hair, and his eyes widened. He gave Martin a startled glance then met Sophia's gaze. "They're here…"

She frowned and leaned closer trying to see what he was talking about. "What are here?"

"My mother's initials. She was afraid one of the children would steal her and scratched her initials along the hairline." He held out the doll, his finger pointed to the tiny crooked letters, *LR*. His finger traced over the shaky letters. "Her name was Luisa Rossi."

"How did you meet Water Lily? Sophia asked.

"I was engaged to marry the daughter of my father's best friend. She was a spoiled child. She told her father I had taken her in a manner unbecoming to a gentleman simply because I wouldn't build her a fancy home like her parents. I was young and had just started as a shipbuilder's apprentice. Her father wouldn't listen to reason and sent the sheriff after me. They caught up with me close to the Cherokee village where I met Water Lily." He shrugged. "You know the rest of the story."

"What happened to the girl?" Martin asked.

"When I returned to Savannah search for Rain Blossom, I heard that she'd fallen from a third-story bedroom terrace and broke her neck."

Sophia was overwhelmed by everything she'd just learned. She turned around, looking for Clay, wanting to share her newfound joy with him…but only Bryan stood there, fidgeting and rocking from foot to foot.

"Bryan? Where has Clay gone?"

"I'm right sorry, Miss Sophia. He left."

Her eyebrows bunched together in confusion. "Well... where did he go?"

Bryan's shoulders slouched, and he dug the toe of one boot into the dirt. "I'm not too sure, ma'am. He was right here as we listened to you folks, and then the next thing I knew, he was gone."

She couldn't decide whether she wanted to scream or cry. Clay had come all this way to help rescue her, and he left without saying anything to her? She pressed her fist over the ache in her chest. "Why did he leave, Martin? I mean, Grandfather." She'd believed Clay had feelings for her, the same feelings she had for him. How could she have been so wrong? She stared at Martin, pleading for an explanation.

The older man cupped her cheek. "Go after him, *u-we-tsi*. You are good for him. For many years, Clay's heart held nothing but hatred and revenge." He smiled, but she saw sadness too. "You have changed his heart, but he feels lost and guilty for not honoring his vow."

She frowned. "But what if..."

Martin shook his head. "You hold his heart, little one. Take my horse and go to him. Follow your own heart, for it will lead you to him."

She leaned in and kissed his wrinkled cheek. Her father was already on his feet, his hand extended to help her up. On impulse, she kissed his cheek as well then turned and ran to the horses. Bryan was already there, holding the reins of a beautiful cream-colored gelding. He offered her a boost, and she quickly settled in the saddle.

"His trail leads that way, Miss Sophia. His horse and this one are herd mates. Trust this one to find the other." Sophia smiled her thanks and clucked to the horse. Gently using her heels, she urged the animal into a trot.

She rode through the darkness, thankful she could see the

trail. She hoped Bryan knew what he was talking about, and her horse knew where he was headed. A couple hours later, as the horizon lightened in the east, her exhaustion turned into excitement. She was positive she was doing the right thing. Her life wouldn't be complete without Clay. She loved him with her whole heart, and she had every intention of telling him so.

In the near distance, a horse whickered, and hers answered. She topped a small hill surrounded by a small grove of trees, and found the remains of a smoldering campfire. Smiling, she gazed through the thinning trail of smoke rising from the logs. Just beyond the charred remains of the fire, she found Clay. He was asleep.

Her heart filled with love as she memorized his handsome face, just as she'd done a thousand times. She loved the rich nutmeg color of his skin, and the way his black hair curled at the ends. Her mouth slowly dipped downward, her smile creeping into a frown as she really looked at him. His skin was more gray than brown and he looked exhausted, even in sleep. She climbed down from her horse, but held onto the hard leather edge of the saddle for support. One last deep breath, and she let go. With each step taking her closer to him, her worry increased.

Squatting down, she touched his shoulder. "Clay?" Silence. She shook his shoulder a little harder. Not even a muscle twitched, and she realized it wasn't a normal sleep. She didn't know what to do. She settled at his side and did the only thing she could. Wait for him to come back to her.

CLAY SOARED ABOVE THE CANOPY, his wings spread wide in his dream shape. Overhead, the night sky appeared brilliant and crisp through the hawk's excellent night vision, but there was still danger here in the dream world. He knew the hawk would keep him safe until he found the answers he searched for.

Cold air riffled through his feathers as he folded his wings against his body and dove lower. Beneath him, the dark expanse of trees stretched like a shadow across the land. Angling the sleek-lined shape of the bird, he cut through a small gap between two large trees and landed on a thick branch covered in gnarled knots. A path appeared below the tree and then divided, running in opposite directions.

The hawk's amazing vision picked out tiny differences along each trail. The left path was darker where murky shadows misted from one tree to another. His spirit walked there, but an oppressive foreboding hung heavy over his heart the longer he walked upon that trail. The farther he traveled, the more labored his heart beat became. Instinctively, he knew only pain and death waited at the end—whether it was his or someone else's, he couldn't tell.

His spirit returned to the path's juncture. The hawk spread his wings and called to the moon. He glanced down the other path, winding away to his right. The moon touched the trees, and his heart lightened, dancing upon the breeze. He inhaled wonderful scents from his childhood. Memories of his mother's fresh bread and roasting meat filled him—smells of a home and family long gone filled his lungs. It beckoned him farther down the path, and he was helpless to resist. As if a hand pushed him faster, he ran onward, seeking its end.

He rounded a corner and stumbled to a stop. He stood in the same clearing where he'd made his camp. The embers of his fire played upon a face so beautiful it took his breath away. His eyes drank in her lush curves before returning to her lovely face. Her long, black hair shimmered in the new day's light. He smiled at the wonderful scene before him—of Sophia's body pressed against his, her head on his shoulder as she slept beside him. He recognized the emotion on her beloved face. It held the same longing, the same depth of feeling he carried in his own heart for her.

Her eyes opened slowly, a sheen of tears shimmering in their rich brown depths. His heart answered with a violent tug as his spirit was wrenched back into his body. He blinked and turned his head. Staring down into her loving eyes, he smiled. He now understood the meaning of his dream. For the first time, true tranquility settled into his heart and mind. Since his family's deaths, he'd found peace.

Overhead, a hawk spiraled against the brilliant blue sky. His call echoed among the trees, and for a moment, neither of them breathed. Turning her gaze back to Clay's smiling face, the knots in her stomach disappeared. She had never seen him so relaxed, as if the heavy weight he carried had disappeared. With a tremulous smile, she cupped his warm cheek with her palm.

"You had me worried," she whispered, afraid the moment would disappear.

"I'm sorry, *tsu-na-da-da-tlu-gi*. I asked the Ancestors to help me find the path I must take."

Her smile faded. The joy of hearing him call her sweetheart dashed as her heart sank. "Your vow to avenge your family?"

One brow rose in surprise. "You knew?"

She nodded. "I asked Martin to tell me. I wanted to know why you seemed so guarded and angry all the time. I thought you didn't like me." Her gaze dropped. "Please don't be mad at him. He didn't want to tell me...said it wasn't his story to tell. But I can be quite persistent when I want to be."

His deep chuckle made her skin feel all warm and tingly. He placed his finger under her chin and raised her face to his. A breath of air rested between their lips. She shivered, wanting to feel them against hers. She inhaled, filling her lungs with his woodsy scent, and a ball of desire pooled low in her womb.

"I have already experienced your persistence—several times," he whispered.

Her cheeks warmed, but the ghost of a smile appeared as she stared at him, willing him to kiss her...love her.

Suddenly, he stood, jerking her from her dreamy state as he grasped her hands and pulled her upright and into his arms. His lips feathered across hers, their pressure growing more insistent. She opened her mouth, and her heart exploded as happiness filled her soul.

He pulled away and smoothed her hair with his hands, his thumbs caressing each cheek. "You are so beautiful, *tsu-na-da-da-tlu-gi*. Your light is a beacon.

"The vow I made was from a grieving son. Because of you, my path lies in a different direction. I choose a life with you—if you'll have me. I want to show you each and every day just how much I love you."

Her eyes widened. She'd dreamed of this moment so many times, and how it would feel to hear those words. Her dreams paled in comparison to the reality. It was magnificent. Her heart soared, and she leaned closer, her chest pressing against the hard expanse of his. Cradling his cheeks between her palms and gently pulled his mouth to hers. The kiss was soft and tender and filled with love.

Clay wrapped his arms tightly around her and deepened the kiss. After a few minutes, she pulled away with a breathless sigh and laid her cheek against his chest, the steady beat of his heart giving her strength. "Leaving Savannah and losing the only family I've ever known tore out my heart. I love you, Clay Jefferson. I know that pain will always be there, but with you by my side, it will fade. Together, we will create new memories…happy memories." She tilted her head back and smiled as happy tears slid down her cheek. With the back of his hand, he tenderly wiped them away.

"I love you, Clay Nighthawk Jefferson. Let me take your pain away as you have mine. Let me fill your future with love."

He picked her up and twirled her around. His whispered reply wrapped lovingly around her heart.

"You already have, my love. You already have."

EPILOGUE

Four years later...

Sophia turned the horse's head back toward the ranch, happier than she'd ever been. Three years had passed since her horrific trip with the Cherokee to their new home in the Indian Territory. So many of her friends had died along the way, but those who had survived had come together, like the family they were, to create their own town. They'd built homes and a school...but most importantly, they'd made wonderful memories to help them forget the terrible ones.

Her smile widened as the steady cadence of another horse galloping behind her drew closer. The rhythmic thudding of the horse's hooves slowed, and she turned her head and gave her husband a sly smile. "I beat you home...again."

Clay grinned, his dark brown eyes filling with amusement. "Only because you cheated."

Sophia's brows rose in what she hoped was an innocent expression. "Me? Cheat?"

Clay's laughter filled the small glen as he leaned over and

pulled her to him for a slow, sweet kiss. "I love you, my beautiful wife."

She kissed him again. "I love you too," she whispered against his full lips. She leaned back in her saddle and gently pressed her heels against the horse's girth as they headed toward their small cabin. "So how did the meeting go with the elders?"

"Just as I thought it would. Usual boring agenda: expanding the township, improving the school building and making it bigger, and finishing up the government complex in the town square. The last building should be completed by the end of the month."

They walked the horses along the trail leading to their home. There were so many trees everywhere, and with the river running along the back of their property, she'd been able to plant a large garden. With Martin's help, of course.

"My friend, Running Fox, also arrived. He will begin training a few men in the ways of the Lighthorse," Clay added. "He's asked me to help."

Sophia's eyes widened. "That's a wonderful idea, Clay! I know how much you miss your work with the Choctaw Lighthorse. Maybe Running Fox can find a place for you within the Cherokee Lighthorse?"

Clay gave her a crooked grin. "I've already been offered the position as head of one unit."

She threw him an annoyed scowl, which disappeared when she heard laughter somewhere ahead of them. "And you weren't even going to ask me first? What if I don't want you risking your life?"

Clay frowned. "I never thought about that…"

Laughing, she brushed the back of her fingers over his smooth cheek. "I'm only joking, Clay. I want you to take the job."

They emerged from the dense trees and walked their

horses toward the corral, stopping by the gate to watch the antics of their young daughter as she ran from Martin, who struggled to catch her. Susan's long black hair streamed behind her as she ran, her little arms pumping to get away. But it was her infectious laughter that filled Sophia's heart with warmth.

She watched as Martin scooped her up into his arms and buried his face against her stomach, making loud noises. Susan laughed harder. When he stopped, she gasped for air and cried out for him to do it again.

She and Clay climbed down from their horses. Sophia watched their precious daughter throw her arms around Martin's neck as he walked back to the porch and his rocking chair. Clay came up behind her and wrapped his arms around her from behind, pulling her back against him. His warm breath tickled her throat as he kissed the tender skin where it curved to join her shoulder.

"Do we need to rescue Martin from our tireless daughter?" Clay asked.

She rested her head against his. "Mmmm. Not just yet. Her great-grandfather will have her napping in no time." She turned in his embrace and wrapped her arms around his neck. "I can think of something I'd much rather do than chase after a precocious three-year-old." She stood on her tiptoes and pressed a tender kiss against his lips.

She stared into his beautiful brown eyes. "I want to show you how much I love you."

Clay traced her cheekbone with the pad of his thumb, his gaze following the invisible path. "I know how much you love me. You show me every moment what's inside your heart." He cupped her face between the palms of his hands and feathered his lips over hers. "Think we can make it to the house without Susan seeing us?"

Sophia giggled. "Probably not, but it will be fun to try."

She gave him a sly smile. "Race you…and whoever loses has to weed the garden for a week!" She turned as if she was going to run and he darted past her, his long strides eating up the distance to the house. She watched Susan launch herself into her father's arms, chattering excitedly about her afternoon adventures.

Tears of happiness filled Sophia's eyes, blurring her vision as she watched her family. She missed the man she still thought of as her father, and had grown close to her real father…but it was the three people before her who made her life complete. Love for her husband, daughter, and grandfather swelled in her chest as she slowly walked toward them. As long as she had them, she would always be home.

∾

I hope you enjoyed *Trail of Hope.* Turn the page to read the excerpt from the next book in the series, *Trail of Courage,* or use the link to buy it.
http://tiny.cc/wt-courage

I need your help.
Reviews help readers find books, so please use the link below to leave a review on Amazon but
BookBub and GoodReads are also great options.
http://www.amazon.com/review/create-review?&asin=B0765PPMJ1

TRAIL OF COURAGE

EXCERPT

Chapter 1

Southeastern Colorado Territory, April 1856

"I am going on that wagon train whether you like it or not." Megan folded her arms over her chest, her stance wide and defiant as she faced her adopted family.

Pa Floyd growled. "Megan Susanne Floyd, we understand you need to find out what happened to yer brother, but our concerns lie with the train. It's too early in the year fer travelin'. You were too young to remember the trip gettin' here. Injun attacks are bad enough, but it's spring. Winter ain't quite over yet, and it usually has a few late surprises. Just when we think it's over, a snowstorm hits. You're takin' a risk, goin' back through Injun country." He pulled on his beard as his anxiety increased. "Don' understand why they're not takin' the Santa Fe Trail."

Megan gave her father a tight smile. "We're traveling southeast to avoid the Kiowa and Comanche war at Sandy Creek. According to Mr. Peabody at the General Store, there should be plenty of water on the southern route. Besides, we've got no choice in the matter. If the train's going south, so are we."

Pa swiped his hand over his mustache and down his grey beard, pulling on it again. "Don't rightly trust that Jones feller none. But Paul's goin' with you. Keep your eyes open wide, Megan girl."

She nodded. "I will, Pa." She glanced at Paul then turned her gaze back to her father, who scratched at his whiskered face. The familiar motion pulled her lips upward. "We will."

"Yer smart enough to know five wagons ain't safe against an Injun attack." Pa stressed his objections in his usual quiet voice. Seeing her knowing grin, he forced his hand down to his side. He nodded toward the small group of people climbing into their wagons at the far end of the wheel-rutted street. "Them folks ain't made from the same stock as most of us out here. They're city folk an' don't belong where every day is a struggle. The law is who draws a gun the fastest. The train leader—that Jones feller—ain't impressed me none at all. He's a mite shifty."

Pa glanced around their small group: his wife, who nodded in agreement with his last statement, and their two oldest sons. His watery gaze rested on the two younger children. "Guess, I shouldn't be callin' either of you children anymore, but," he pulled his wife to his side. "You know your ma and I always thought of you as our own, and we're right proud of how the two of you have grown up." He stood a little straighter and gave Megan and Paul a quick nod. "Right proud."

Megan fidgeted with the small satchel in her hands. She knew she was different from most women and didn't fit in with proper folks. Her long, black braid, honey-colored skin, and dark brown eyes let everyone know she was Indian, although from what tribe remained a mystery. She also knew her adopted father was worried about how the people in

Arkansas and Tennessee would react to her asking questions about her murdered parents. It was her older brother, Clay, she wanted to learn about. What had happened to him? Why had he never tried to find her?

She caught Paul's gaze and gave him a tiny smile. His sun-bleached brown hair curled against the short collar of his off-white shirt, and his fingers worried the brim of his worn, brown slouch hat. Pa was right. Paul had grown into a respectable young man. His story was so like hers but worse. Her parents had been taken from her while his father and brother had left him behind to die. Because they shared such a similar past, they had bonded almost immediately. One night when she'd caught him crying, he confided to her that his mother had also been killed—like hers had.

In an unaccustomed move, Paul grabbed hold of Megan's hand, his pale green eyes staring down at her. "If this is what you need to do..."

"It is." Megan wanted to cry. These people had taken her in when she was a ten-year-old child and raised her as their own. They were good people—but this trip was too important to her. Searching for her brother at the Mississippi River landing in Eastern Arkansas was vital. Before she could move on with her life, she had to know what had happened to him...uncertainty about his fate had followed her for seventeen years. Still, a part of her felt guilty, as if she were betraying the Floyds and all they'd done for her.

Boots clapped on the boarded sidewalk and stopped behind her. Whoever it was cleared his throat. "Miss Floyd, the wagon train's ready to head out. If'n we want to make the pass by night, we can't tarry any longer."

Megan turned and offered the scruffy mountain man a smile. "Thank you, Mr. Jones. Mr. Daniels and I won't be long." He hobbled back down the sidewalk and stepped off into the muddy street, heading toward the small cluster of wagons next to the livery stable.

She followed the line of storefronts with her gaze. Shopkeepers and customers bustled in and out of the buildings as they went about their daily lives. She'd worked in her father's trading post for years and knew most of these people. They were her friends.

With a sigh, she turned back to her family, their faces pinched with worry. She pressed a fist over the ache in her chest. "I'm sorry…"

Ma Floyd threw her arms around Megan's neck and held on tight for a few moments then dropped her arms and stepped away. "Okay, now. I'm a mite worried 'bout you agoin' with them city folk—don't even know how t' properly shoot a gun. But you're a good girl. Smart and steady goin'. And you'll have Paul travelin' along to protect you as well. Go. Find your brother, then come on back home. Both o' you."

"You keep yer eyes and ears open, li'l sis." Seth's deep voice rumbled. "There's Injun trouble everywhere."

"Mind your rifles, and make sure you have plenty of ammunition. Stock up at Fort Gibson, even if you don't run into any trouble. You can never have enough," Tom added, his voice a bit more gravelly than usual.

Through her tears, Megan offered a shaky smile. Turning, she walked toward the wagon train and an unknown future.

~

Will the harsh frontier and wild weather tear Megan and Bryan apart or will the hope of love and family keep them together? To find out, go to the link below.

TRAIL OF COURAGE

http://tiny.cc/wt-courage

AUTHOR'S NOTES

As a historical researcher, not to mention very OCD, I have to have my facts straight or I simply can't sleep at night; however, there's also the sticky point of making the story work as well.

Most people don't know a lot about the Tribe relocations that took place over a ten-year span. They were a travesty no matter how you look at them. Too many people died and so much of their cultures lost. My Choctaw hero and his family moved to Indian Territory in the early 1830s and were fairly well situated by the time the last Cherokee removal took place. Sophia and Martin experienced that removal, which began in 1838 and ended in 1839. Believe it or not, there were seven different routes the military used to transport the tribes from the eastern states to their new homes in Indian Territory, which, as we all know, later became my home state of Oklahoma.

The winter of 1838-1839 was also one of the worst in decades with more freezing temperatures, snow, and ice—

even in the states where snow rarely happened. We've seen this very thing during the last decade. Who would ever have thought that Atlanta, GA would be completely shut down because of snow and ice?

Another point I tried to show in this story was the difference between the plains tribes, usually shown on TV wearing loincloth and feathers and living in teepees, and the eastern tribes, who weren't like that at all. They dressed the same as the White population's different class structure—the workers wore working clothes and the rich wore suits and gowns. The Cherokee also lived in clapboard homes and had well-situated communities as well as college graduates with prestigious careers that included doctors, and lawyers. For the most part, thanks to Sequoyah, who created the Cherokee alphabet, they could read and write where a lot of the White settlers could not.

Did you know the sole purpose for moving the tribes was because of their land and its riches: fertile farmland, forests, precious metals, and gemstones? In my opinion, greed will always be the root of all evil.

If you love historical romances, sign up for my reader list, and as a thank you, I'll send you the prequel, a novella, in my Western Trails series.

To download, go to http://tiny.cc/nl-histwest

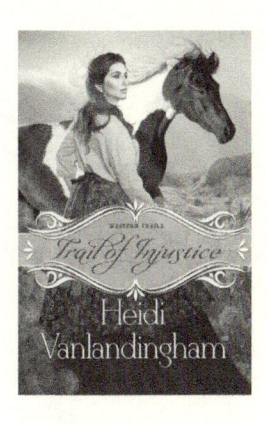

LUCIE: BRIDE OF TENNESSEE

PREQUEL, MAIL-ORDER BRIDES OF THE SOUTHWEST

http://tiny.cc/mobsw-amob-lucie

To provide for herself and her younger brother, Lucie Croft accepts a mail-order bride contract in Chattanooga. Fate has other things in store for her when her intended groom dies before her arrival. Desperate and homeless, Lucie relies on the kindness of a local hotel owner, Sebastian McCord. Overwhelmed as a single father and intrigued by Lucie, Sebastian agrees to marry her. Will the couple create a loving family or does fate have yet another turn in the road?

This book is also #16 in the American Mail-Order Brides series.

ALSO BY HEIDI VANLANDINGHAM

IN READING ORDER

For all Buy Links: www.heidivanlandingham.com

Western Trails

Trail of Hope

Trail of Courage

Trail of Secrets

Mia's Misfits

Mia's Misfits is also in ABC Mail-Order Bride series

Trail of Redemption

American Mail-Order Bride series &
Prequel to Mail-Order Brides of the Southwest

Lucie: Bride of Tennessee

Mail-Order Brides of the Southwest

The Gambler's Mail-Order Bride

The Bookseller's Mail-Order Bride

The Marshal's Mail-Order Bride

The Woodworker's Mail-Order Bride

The Gunslinger's Mail-Order Bride

The Agent's Mail-Order Bride

WWII

Heart of the Soldier

Flight of the Night Witches

Night Witch Reborn: Natalya

The Peacemaker: Aleksandra

The Warrior Queen: Raisa

The Last Night Witch: Lilyann

Kingdom of the Elf Lords

Return of the Elf Lord

Coming 2022

The Elf Lord's Curse

Of Mystics and Mayhem

In Mage We Trust

Saved By the Spell

The Curse That Binds

Mistletoe Kisses

Music and Moonlight

Sleighbells and Snowflakes

Angels and Ivy

Nutcrackers and Sugarplums

Box Sets Available

Mail-Order Brides of the Southwest: 3-Book collection

Mistletoe Kisses: 4-book collection

Western Trails: 2-book collection

ABOUT THE AUTHOR

Author Heidi Vanlandingham writes sweet, action-packed stories that take place in the Wild West, war-torn Europe, and otherworldly magical realms. Her love of history finds its way into each book, and her characters are lovable, strong, and diverse.

Growing up in Oklahoma and living one year in Belgium gave Heidi a unique perspective regarding different cultures. She still lives in Oklahoma with her husband and youngest son. Her favorite things in life are laughter, paranormal romance books, music, and long road trips.

Heidi currently writes multiple genres but mostly fixates on fantasy/paranormal and historical romance.

For more about Heidi: www.heidivanlandingham.com

- amazon.com/Heidi-Vanlandingham/e/B00BI5NPA8?tag=heidivanlaaut-20
- bookbub.com/authors/heidi-vanlandingham
- goodreads.com/heidivanlandingham
- facebook.com/heidi.vanlandingham.author
- instagram.com/heidivanlandingham_author
- pinterest.com/Hvanlandingham

Made in United States
North Haven, CT
16 October 2024

59017753R00093